ATILUS THE GLADIATOR

Borgo Press Books by E. C. Tubb

Assignment New York: A Mike Lantry Classic Crime Novel
Enemy of the State: Fantastic Mystery Stories
Galactic Destiny: A Classic Science Fiction Tale
The Ming Vase and Other Science Fiction Stories
Mirror of the Night and Other Weird Tales
Only One Winner: Science Fiction Mystery Tales
Sands of Destiny: A Novel of the French Foreign Legion
Star Haven: A Science Fiction Tale
Tomorrow: Science Fiction Mystery Tales
The Wager: Science Fiction Mystery Tales
The Wonderful Day: Science Fiction Stories

THE ATILUS TRILOGY

1. *Atilus the Slave*
2. *Atilus the Gladiator*
3. *Atilus the Lanista*

ATILUS THE GLADIATOR

THE SAGA OF ATILUS, BOOK TWO: AN HISTORICAL NOVEL

E. C. TUBB

THE BORGO PRESS

MMXIII

ATILUS THE GLADIATOR

FIRST BORGO PRESS EDITION

Published by Wildside Press LLC
www.wildsidebooks.com

DEDICATION

To the memory of Iris Kathleen, née Smith

CONTENTS

CHAPTER ONE

He was small, barely five feet, his tunic soiled and his eyes brimming with tears. A forlorn little figure lost in the crowd and frightened by the noise. Down the road sweating slaves hauled carts bearing caged animals, men who were accustomed to the stench and who were more docile than the oxen normally used for such work. Beside them strode overseers, their whips busy, lacing naked flesh with stripes of red.

'Move!' A *bestiarius*, impatient at the delay, came to roar at the cartiers. 'Those beasts have to be settled in before noon if you hope for sport tomorrow. Where's the agent? Tamillius, I'll have your hide unless you hurry. You're late as it is.'

'Am I to blame for the disfavour of the gods?' Tamillius, a tall man wearing a soiled garment, his face strained and savage, halted facing the *bestiarius*. 'Twice we have suffered broken wheels. Three times the beasts had to be watered. You gave me insufficient time and winds delayed the vessel. May Jupiter bear witness that I tell the truth.'

'To Hades with your excuses. Get those animals to the arena. They—' The *bestiarius* broke off at the sound of a scream. 'The fool!'

A slave, staggering with fatigue, had stepped too close to one of the cages. It held a lion which struck out with a taloned paw. Blood spurted from lacerated flesh, skin and muscles ripped from a shoulder, a carmine flood staining the unfortunate man's body, falling to dapple the dusty road.

'Get him away from there!' The *bestiarius* lunged forward.

'Don't poke at the lion, you fools! That animal is worth a dozen such scum. Tamillius, get moving!'

Noise and confusion augmented by the crack of whips and the snarls of the caged beasts unsettled at the scent of blood. A sound punctuated by the laughter of the crowd as the injured man was carried away. A normal scene in any small town on the eve of a *munera* and a promise of what was to be offered during the gladiatorial display.

Dropping to one knee, I stared at the boy.

'Your name, son?'

'Please, sir, Marcus.' He sniffed, trying hard not to cry. 'My father is Valerius Harpius and he owns a shop close to the market.'

'And your mother, boy?'

'We were together and then the animals came and some men got between us. I looked for her, but...' Tears rolled down the cheeks. 'I looked and looked but couldn't find her.'

Even now she would be looking for him, but the lad was small and the crowd thick. Rising, I looked around and saw a vendor of comestibles. With a sticky, honeyed bun clutched in his hand I lifted the boy to my shoulder and turned so that he could see what was going on in the road.

The carts were rumbling on their way, a group of *bestiarii* following them, smiling and waving at the crowd. They were scarred men who fought wild beasts on the sand, sometimes with bare hands, but more often with sword or spear. One of them recognised me and called a greeting.

'Ave, Atilus! You fighting tomorrow?'

'Yes.'

'Then good luck, friend.'

'And to you, Pollidor.'

The crowd closed in as they passed, men making comments as to the number and condition of the animals, some scornful of what they had seen.

'Lions,' said one. 'Why not tigers? I know they're expensive, but it's time the *duumvir* put on a decent show.'

'There'll be dogs too,' said his companion. 'And some bulls. I was having a drink with a *bestiarius* last night and he told me. These animals are a last-minute addition.'

'Dogs and bulls!' The man shrugged. 'Why, in Rome they have ostriches and bears, antelopes and wolves, rhinoceroses and even crocodiles. There you can be sure of getting a decent show.'

'This is Aricia, not Rome, so be thankful for what you get. Anyway, the gladiators are good. They've got Leacus and Andrax as well as Atilus—'

'Atilus Cindras?'

'That's the one. You ever see him fight? A wizard with a sword and about the best *secutor* there is. If you're thinking of making a wager, then he's the one to back.'

'Maybe.' The other sucked in his cheeks. 'But if he's so good, then why isn't he fighting in Rome?'

A comment I had heard before and now, as then, ignored. With the boy riding on my shoulder I walked along the street towards the market, the lad clearly visible to any who might be looking.

'Marcus!' The woman who came running towards me had a plain and faded face, her figure slight beneath her stola. 'Marcus, thank the gods I've found you!'

'I've been watching the animals.' He wriggled as I set him down. 'Mother, this is Atilus. He's a famous gladiator.'

I saw her smile turn to a frown. Gladiators were a necessary evil and she, probably the daughter of some strict household, would have been taught to despise them. Yet even so she was polite.

'Atilus.' Her head inclined a little. 'I must thank you for looking after the boy.'

'A fine lad. You must be proud of him.'

'I am.' Firmly she took his hand in her own. 'Now come, Marcus, and say nothing of this to your father. You know how strict he can be at times.'

The Romans were addicted to the harsh traditions of the past.

The sting of a rod would teach the lad to be more obedient, but, watching as they walked from where I stood, I doubted if it would be given. A held tongue and his mother's lie would see to that. The normal way of a normal life—one of which I had no part.

As I had no real part in the event taking place in the house at which I was a guest.

Sentonius Papirus was the local Master of Games, and normally at such a time would have been busy at the amphitheatre, but today was a special occasion. His daughter, Bellitia, was to be married, and I had been invited to the ceremony.

She was a lovely girl, her beauty more than compensating for the limited dowry her father was able to provide, and Antonius, her betrothed, was a fortunate man. Together they stood before the minor priest as the wedding contract was read and duly witnessed, and then, taking her by the wrist, he made a show of dragging her from the paternal home. She resisted him, smiling, wearing her best clothes, her hair neatly dressed, the brightly coloured scarf over her shoulders accentuating its ebon sheen. As we clapped and cheered she finally yielded, stepping outside to be showered with walnuts from waiting children, then to be taken to her new home, there to be carried over the threshold.

'A happy day,' said Sentonius as they departed. 'Well, friends, wine and food is waiting. A toast first to bless the couple.'

We drank, first spilling a few drops on the floor of the *atrium* with its decorative mosaics as a libation to the gods. It was good wine. Sentonius hadn't stinted on the provisions for the feast, and he came to thank me for the gift I had given to the young couple.

'A lamp of silver chased with gold. You were generous, Atilus. It will be useful.'

'To light their way to bed?'

'Who wants light for that?' His seamed face split into a grin. 'This day in nine months' time I'll be a grandfather, or I don't know my daughter. May the gods grant them a son.'

'I'll drink to that.'

Delia joined us as we lowered our goblets. No longer young, she was still a handsome woman, her face bearing the traces of the beauty which had drawn Sentonius to make her his wife.

'What's wrong with girls?' she demanded. 'Always you men wish for sons yet, unless there are girls, who will mother them? Would you want nothing but sons, Atilus?'

Remembering the recent weight on my shoulder I said, 'One son would be nice, Domina.'

'And would you expect it to be hatched from an egg?'

'Hardly.' I returned her smile. 'I would like it to be born from a woman as lovely as yourself.'

'Flatterer!' Her eyes examined me. 'You talk as well as you fight. Husband, it is time for you to circulate among our guests.'

'Must I?' Sentonius scowled. 'You know how I hate empty chatter, and I should be at the amphitheatre. There are things waiting my attention.'

'They can wait. This is your daughter's wedding day and courtesy is expected of you. Hurry now and tend your guests. At least receive their congratulations—and don't forget to smile.' She sighed as he moved reluctantly through the crowd. 'Why are men such cowards, Atilus? I've seen Sentonius face a crazed slave with naked hands, and yet he flinches from social encounters such as this. If your daughter had been married, would you act the same?'

'I have no daughter.'

'No daughter, no son, no wife, no home.' Her hand fell to rest lightly on my arm. 'Doesn't the lack of these things trouble you at times? A man should be married, Atilus. It is the natural order of things.'

My goblet was empty and I gestured to a passing slave to replenish it, sipping at the strong, ruby wine. It was an excuse for not answering the question and one the woman recognised.

'I have known many gladiators since marrying Sentonius,' she said quietly, 'but there are few I would welcome in my house. You are one of those few. And there was something in your eyes when you watched the ceremony, an ache, a yearning, something of which you were perhaps unaware, but it was there. Have you never, ever thought of settling down?'

Again I remembered the weight on my shoulder, the warm comfort of the small, sturdy shape. It would be good to have a son, to teach, to watch grow, to become an extension of myself. But I was a gladiator, and how could such a thing be?

I had seen them too often, the women who had joined their lives to those who fought in the arena. The women and the children they had borne to their men. Standing, waiting, watching with haunted eyes, never knowing if this time he would fail to return. Never being sure that, even if he did, he wouldn't be maimed and crippled, blinded and helpless, forced to drag out his life as a beggar in the streets.

What future was that to offer any woman?

What kind of father to offer to a son?

The wine was rich and sweet, but suddenly it held a bitter sourness so that I put aside the goblet. In the arena a man had no friends. In the world he could have no dependents. A gladiator lived from one fight to another, and only the gods knew how long he could continue. Delia must know that, but weddings made some women a little mad and turned them into determined match-makers. And yet, from her, I had expected better.

'Atilus, I'm sorry.' With swift intuition she had guessed my thoughts. 'You must forgive me. It's just that I—well, I hate to see waste. And, if you go down, what a waste that would be.'

Her hand closed on my arm. 'Please, friend, you will forgive me?'

'For what, Domina?' I smiled, staring into her eyes. 'For being kind?'

'For being thoughtless. You fight tomorrow and must have nothing on your mind.'

Nothing but the determination to kill the man I would face.

CHAPTER TWO

Aricia was a small town set on the Appian Way, a place with few of the comforts and distractions of Rome. A farming community, the town was ringed with the villas and estates of the wealthy, absentee landlords leaving the management of their property to trusted agents. The amphitheatre itself, built in a natural hollow, was constructed of wood and stone. Like the town, it was small, the actual arena little more than a hundred feet long by eighty wide, the tiered stands now filled with those who had come to witness the games.

It was past noon and the preliminaries were over. The beasts which had been hauled from the port at Tarracina were dead, together with those already installed, and the crowd, blood-lust wetted, tore the air with strident yells.

'Atilus! Atilus Cindras! Get him, man! Kill! Kill!'

I ignored the shouts, not looking at the packed *maeniana*; the avid spectators. With a man like Leacus it would be suicide to give him such an opportunity.

He was a Cappadocian with all the sly cunning of his breed, a *retiarius*, arrogant and confident of victory. Now, edging towards me, he purred the traditional chant.

'I do not hunt you. I seek a fish. Why do you swim away, Atilus?'

The net in his hand twitched as he spoke, the mesh weighted with gilded pellets of lead. Held in his other hand, the barbs of the *fascina* caught and reflected the sunlight from points and edges. The trident with its long shaft, which he used with the skill of long familiarity.

Naked aside from a leather belt and apron, his skin held an oiled sheen. A thin, metal fillet confined his hair and the only armour he wore, the *galerus* strapped to his left shoulder, was ornamented with embossed designs of fish and crabs.

A lithe man, he was fast and dangerous, filled with the determination to kill. A determination matched by my own.

Today either he or I would spill our lives on the sand.

'Are you afraid of me, Atilus?' he purred. 'Listen to the crowd shouting for you. How will they shout, I wonder, when you are down and begging for mercy? Down and dying with my barbs buried in your guts.'

Talk to distract the attention as was the turn of the trident he held, the sunlight blazing from the polished tines. The net hissed towards my feet over the sand, a simple move and one easy to avoid, yet had I not anticipated it, the mesh would have wound itself around my ankle and a sharp tug could have brought me down.

Springing over it I backed, wary, the shield held close to my left side, my left leg with its protective greave thrust forward. The helmet, wide-brimmed, visored with a perforated plate which covered my face, was heavy, and sweat ran down into my eyes despite the wad of padding. Like the *retiarius* I wore a belt and leather apron, but had no dagger. My only weapon was the *gladius* which I held as an extension of my armoured right arm.

Too much armour and yet not enough. It slowed movement, yet failed to give complete protection. My thighs, torso, and right leg were bare. My left arm, my throat, my back from neck to ankles. Only by facing Leacus could I hope to defend myself from the thrust of his trident. Only by dodging could I escape from the cast of his net.

It came like a cloud against the clear blue of the sky, opening, spreading as it fell, the mesh wide to engulf my helmet, my upper arms. To catch and throw it aside with the shield would be to expose my body to the threat of the trident. To beat at it with my sword was to turn and give the barbs a defenceless target.

Moving quickly to the left I ducked, swung the *gladius* in a sharp circle, felt the impact of the strands and moved in with a sudden lunge.

Time and skill were against me. Leacus was already on the retreat, pulling the net after him with the thong which attached it to his wrist. My shield barely missed his hand, and my sword, thrusting, caught the net. Tearing it free I caught a glimpse of stabbing barbs through the eye-holes of my visor. Lowering my head I took the blow on my helmet, feeling the tug of the strap beneath my chin as the tines hit hard against the crest. Again I struck, an upward sweeping blow this time, and felt the grate as the edge rasped on the withdrawn barbs. A quick move forward and I sent the steel hissing through the air in a slashing cut.

'Habet!' The crowd yelled as blood traced a path over the oiled torso. *'Habet!'*

Leacus was wounded and knew it. He had felt the impact, the burn, saw the blood which fell from the wound to stain his thighs, the sand beneath his feet. Turning, he ran to put distance between us, halting to face me, chest heaving, lips thinned in a snarl.

'Atilus! ' screamed a woman. 'Get him! Kill him—and take me for a prize!'

'Open his belly,' yelled a plump senator, his face like his voice, distorted with passion. 'Slice his guts!'

They were impatient, eager for the kill, but to rush in was to risk too much. The *retiarius* was barely scratched; blood made the shallow gash appear worse than it was, and he was waiting and ready. Yet it would be a mistake to wait too long. As a secutor, my part was to chase the other, to be the 'pursuer' in our combat. A disadvantage to add to the rest.

Always the *retiarius* had the greater chance. The net, the reach of the trident, his greater mobility, all were in his favour, the odds being five to three. Yet despite that, a *retiarius* was held in low esteem. Romans loved the sword, the *gladius* which had given them the world, the weapon with which they had cut their way to an empire.

And, loving it, they wanted to see it used.

'In!' they screamed. 'Atilus! In!'

Both veterans of the arena, we had no attendant trainers or slaves waiting to lash and burn us into combat. A fact appreciated by the *cognoscenti*, who took a delight in the skill displayed by experienced fighters, and who argued for hours over the relative merits of various weapons. Dilettantes who claimed to see a beauty in combat, but who had never experienced it from the viewpoint of those engaged. For those in the arena things were different.

On the sand life could hang on a trifle. A patch of hidden blood or excreta on which a foot could slip, a momentary hesitation, a mistake in judgement, a mistimed blow, all could cost a man his life. Small things, but death waited on such.

And death was always waiting.

It came at me in a glitter of points, a mist-like swirl of a thrown mesh. Pellets rapped against the brim of my helmet and the metal of my visor tore as, dodging the net, I was slow to avoid the trident. Luck was with me; had I not turned in time, had the thrust been delivered with greater force, the barbs would have ripped through the bronze to reach my eyes.

Dropping to one knee I slashed at the long, muscular legs. My shield jerked as the net, pulled free, caught at the metal. Like an asp the trident thrust at the exposed flesh, the tines clashing against my blocking sword. Locked together, both weapons rose as I reared upright. For a moment we stood face to face, then Leacus had torn free and was backing.

Any *retiarius* knew the value of distance. It was his greatest advantage and the one thing a *secutar* had to overcome if he hoped to win. To get in close within the reach of the trident, to get into sword-range in order to cut and thrust at the unprotected body, to use the shield and helmet to full advantage.

'Atilus! In man, in!'

'Snare him, Leacus! Bring him down!'

The roar of the crowd was like the sound of distant surf and voices blended one into the other, words indistinguishable, the thunder a feral baying, a savage demand for blood.

To wait was to allow the *retiarius* to recover. To attack was to take a chance, but one which could be minimized. Weaving, feinting, I watched the hands, the feet, calling on hard-won experience to anticipate what Leacus would do next and to plan accordingly.

A fighter develops certain characteristics, using tactics which have served him well in the past, and Leacus was no exception. Already I had learned that he twitched his hand twice before casting the net and that he favoured an overhand use of the trident. Tall, he could afford to lift it high and thrust downwards, but I too was tall, a fact he had apparently overlooked.

Deliberately I crouched a little, lessening my height, planning even as I edged towards him. To get in, to tempt him to make a downward thrust, to move fast enough to get inside the reach of the tines and then to suddenly rear, catching the shaft on my shoulder, to lift the *gladius* and beat it aside.

And then, with luck, a moment in which he would be at my mercy.

A gamble, and one which would have to be conducted with care. Leacus was experienced, the winner of many combats, a *primus palus*, a first-class fighter. No *tyro*, he would not be easy to delude.

'Atilus,' he said. 'The next time, you bastard, I'll get you. The barbs in your guts, twisting, pulling out your tripes. I'll ruin that pretty body of yours.'

Had he a plan of his own? If so, what?

I had dropped and cut at his legs, tempting him with a wide-flung shield. He had lunged—was that it?

His net had caught my shield and he had not run as he should have done. A mistake or a calculated feint? I had no time to judge, instinct would decide.

I advanced, watching distance, slowing as I saw the twitch of his hand. Once...twice...the net rose like a web, spreading as it fell, the weights at the edges holding it wide and dragging it down.

A good throw, but I was ready and waiting. Crouching I lifted my shield and ducked under the near edge, felt the weights rap on my helmet and back as, like lightning, the net closed and the trident came darting at my throat

Already I was moving.

Sand gritted beneath my sandals as I lunged forward following the pull of the net. Tines rasped on the metal protecting my right shoulder and glanced from it as I rose to my full height, a swing of my sword knocking it aside. Leacus was fast. I saw his eyes widen with sudden fear and caught the blur of his net hand as he snatched at the dagger in his belt. Caught in the net, my shield was useless. My sword was too far to one side; before I could bring it to bear, he would have the dagger in action, steel driving between my ribs, into my unprotected stomach. Only one thing was left for me to do.

Lifting my left shin, I slammed it upwards between his thighs.

Shin, not foot, we were too close for that. The greave was a hammer catching him in the crotch and crushing his testicles. Before me his face changed, became suffused with agony as he staggered backwards, doubled, retching.

A blow from the flat of my sword sent him to sprawl helpless on the sand.

'Atilus!' The crowd rose, shouting. 'Atilus!'

The moment of victory, always sweet. The gamble won, and I had lived and would fight again. Kicking aside the trident and dagger, I rested my foot on the neck of the fallen man. An elementary precaution; though hurt, it was still possible for him to roll clear, snatch up a weapon and reverse the victory. If he tried, I would kill him, a messy end which would not please the crowd, which liked to deliver the final verdict. Beneath my sandal Leacus groaned as, sweating, he extended one arm and raised his forefinger in a plea for mercy.

He deserved it. He had fought well and had done his best, but the decision was not up to me. Lifting the *gladius* I looked to where the editor of the games sat in his ornate chair on the podium.

Quinctius Pullvillius was a *duumvir* of Aricia, a sleekly plump man, part of whose duties was to provide gladiatorial displays, and who intended to get full value from this particular *munera*. And yet it had fallen short of the expectations of the crowd. The *trinqui* had been few; only a handful of sacrificial victims were thrown to the beasts, and the *bestiarii* had not been of the best. Leacus and I had been the prime entertainment but, according to the crowd, he had put up a bad show.

'Lugula!' They screamed. 'Kill!'

The editor had the final say. If the crowd had demanded mercy by a display of fluttering handkerchiefs and uplifted thumbs, he would have gone against their wishes to his later, political cost. Now, to grant mercy would earn the same reward. For a moment he hesitated, then, lifting his arm, he let it fall to extend before him, the thumb downturned in the signal for death.

Leacus saw it. Gasping he said, 'Atilus—'

He died as my sword plunged into his heart.

CHAPTER THREE

Heraculis came running to meet me as I walked through the Gate of Life. The wine he carried was welcome and I drank it after throwing him my helmet. On the way to the preparation room he babbled, 'A good fight, master, but twice I thought the gods had summoned you for their own. Yet my prayers were answered and you survived.'

I made no answer, sitting on a bench as he removed the greave. The man was a mongrel, with the traces of mixed parentage blended in his face and eyes. A small, wizened man who at times looked like an ancient monkey. His name was a joke, one he had adopted, I guessed, as a compensation for his diminutive size. A slave who had been offered for sale after taking one too many liberties with his master. I had bought him cheap and at times regretted it.

Now, as he swabbed the dust and sweat from my body with a sponge, I heard the sudden sharp intake of his breath.

'A near thing, master.' I felt a twinge of pain as his fingers pressed at a point to the side of my neck. 'A cut,' he explained. 'Nothing serious, but had it been an inch to one side, you and not Leacus would have been dragged from the sand.'

A near miss: one of the barbs glancing from my armoured shoulder had torn the flesh. A minor wound which would probably heal without leaving a scar, for which I was grateful. Most gladiators were proud of their wounds, displaying their scars as a legionary showed his medallions, but I was not one of them. Scars I had, no fighter could escape them, but the one on my left cheek, the others on side and shoulder, the cicatrices on my thighs, were enough.

As Heraculis reached for gum to plug the gash I said, 'Leave it. It will heal faster left exposed.'

'As you wish, master.' His shrug was expressive. 'But don't blame me if it festers.'

'It won't.'

'I shall burn incense to the gods of healing to make sure of that, master. Another sacrifice to add to the others I have made on your behalf.' Slyly he added, 'It hasn't been easy. Even a few *sesterces* is a large sum to a poor slave.'

'You can afford it.'

'But how, master?' His hands spread in a gesture born in the east. 'Am I a freedman to be paid a wage? Where would I get money to call my own?'

'From me,' I said bluntly. 'From the extra you add to the bills, and from the bribes you take from those asking questions as to my prospect of victory. Do you take me for an idiot?'

'Master, you are wisdom personified! How could any mortal man hope to delude you? Perhaps a few coins have come my way from those interested in your progress, but they have been well spent, master. And all I have is yours.'

The matter wasn't worth pursuing. All slaves cheated as a matter of course, and Heraculis was an expert at the art. Now, as he fastened my sandals, he said, 'The baths, master?'

'The baths.'

Always after a fight I liked to wash, to remove the dirt and grime and to ease the tension of nerve and muscle. The sponging had helped, but hadn't been enough, and the amphitheatre, poorly equipped, offered nothing better than a tub of sun-warmed water, oil, and pumice. And, if Aricia had nothing else to commend it, the baths were superb.

They were of stone faced with marble, the gift of a rich merchant who had dedicated them to the god Augustus almost a century earlier. The attendants were mostly Greeks, young slaves deft and amiable. The *unctores* were skilled in their trade, supple fingers massaging aches from bone and sinew.

Heraculis had accompanied me as was his duty. Now he scowled at the attendants as he draped my discarded clothing over his arm.

'Greeks,' he muttered. 'Have a care, master, such will sap your strength given half a chance.'

'So?'

'You're prime bait for what they offer—but if you want to indulge, why waste your time on such as these? There are three men I could name who would pay well for your company. Two knights and—'

'Watch your tongue, Heraculis!'

'—a senator,' he continued blandly. 'Once, when the tines almost speared you, I saw one wince. Of them all, he would be the most generous.'

'As I will be,' I snapped, 'with a whip unless you learn to mind your manners.'

'Master, I apologise.' His bow was a mockery. 'Beat my old bones if it pleases you—but will my blood wash away the truth? A fighter like yourself, as handsome as Apollo and with a body to match: are men stone that they do not appreciate what they see? One night with the senator and you could gain as much as you won in the arena today.'

With a fat commission for himself, no doubt. I stared at him where he stood, then broke into a smile. The man was incorrigible, and it was proof of his cunning that he had managed to live so long. Old, without physical strength, he had used his brains and shrewdness to survive. A trait I could appreciate.

'You'd sell me like a hunk of meat, Heraculis. You should have been a pander.'

'Once, in Syria, master, I was. There I learned how to gain from the vices of men. Of women too,' he added thoughtfully. 'But the gods did not see fit to give me natural advantages and, well, luck was against me.'

Bad fortune in the shape of the legions, the uprising they quelled, his being taken among the captives sold as slaves. A thing we had in common.

'Master?'

'No.' Greek love had never appealed to me. 'I'll be at least an hour. Go to the house of Senontius Papirus and collect our things. Find a lodging in some tavern.'

'We are leaving, master?'

'The house, yes.' I'd already made my farewells and sensed that, perhaps, I'd stayed too long. Too long in the sense that I had begun to feel a stranger, and the wedding had firmed my decision. Delia, understanding, had been gentle. Sentonius, gruff, had agreed that it was time for me to move on. And he had dropped a hint which had confirmed a growing suspicion.

'Be careful, Atilus,' he'd said. 'Some lanistae aren't to be wholly trusted, but I don't have to tell you that. I've nothing against Arrius Clemens, but, well, maybe you've been with him too long.'

A warning which I intended to take.

Naked, my body coated with scented olive oil, I went into the *caladarium* where Arrius sat relaxing in the heat. The *lanista* was a big, bulky man now running to fat, his body seamed with ancient scars. Once a gladiator, he had almost died from a wound which had forced him to limp for the rest of his life. Unable to fight, he had gathered a troupe of gladiators and now moved around the provinces with his *familia*. I had joined him almost a year ago.

'Atilus!' He gestured at me through a cloud of steam. 'Sit beside me and take some of the ache from your bones. I know how it is.'

I sat beside him, breathing deeply, letting the heated vapour enter my lungs. Sweat mingled with the oil on my body, smarting a little as it stung the shallow wound.

'You fought well,' said Arrius. 'Leacus was a good man and deserved better than he got. But what do you expect in places like this? Skill means nothing, all they want is blood.'

'Couldn't something have been arranged?'

'I tried, but you know how Leacus was. Overconfident and

his *lanista* wouldn't co-operate. The man is a fool.'

And the loser because of it. The prize could have been shared, the *charonian* whose task it was to check the fallen and make certain they were dead could have been bribed to restrain the hammer with which he crushed the skulls of the wounded. A surface cut which provided plenty of blood, but which would have done no real harm, would have deluded the crowd. Leacus would have lived to fight again.

Perhaps he had expected to live. I remembered his dying gasp, the expression in his eyes as my sword had plunged home. But if an arrangement had been made, I'd known nothing of it.

Arrius rubbed an old scar. It writhed over the upper part of his right thigh and up halfway across his stomach. The wound which had crippled him for life.

'Did I ever tell you how I got this?' He pressed on without waiting for my answer. 'A mistake I made at Pompeii during the time of Emperor Claudius. The god Claudius, I should say, since he was deified by the Senate. It was about the time he invaded Britain, which would make it,' he paused, 'thirteen years ago now.'

'Sixteen,' I corrected.

'As long ago as that?' Arrius shrugged. 'Well, time flies as they say, but are you sure?'

I had reason to remember.

When the Romans had invaded Britain under the personal command of Claudius, I had been a boy of ten. A child of the Iceni who had stood with his mother in the stronghold at Brentwood with the assembled forces under Caractacus. The legions had beaten us and made Britain with its treasures a province of Rome. My mother had been raped and murdered. I had been taken captive and sold into slavery. A servitude which had lasted eleven years. Which had ended only when, as a gladiator-slave, I had won the *rudis*, Nero himself handing me the symbolical wooden sword, together with my freedom.

'A mistake,' said Arrius, determined to tell his story. 'The worst I ever made. Take my advice, Atilus and never forget to sacrifice to the gods before entering the arena. I didn't and, each time I take a step now, I'm reminded of my negligence by the gods I ignored. The gods and Malcenus.'

Again he rubbed at his scar and I wondered why he was telling me this. Talk, to some men, is a mask, a means to hide their thoughts. To others it is a weapon, a way to lull and to delude. We had never been close and I was suspicious of his sudden friendliness.

'Malcenus,' said Arrius. 'He was one of a pair of *postulati* fighting in full armour, armed with a sword and lead mace and willing to take on all-comers with the weapons of their choice. I was a *retiarius* then, though you wouldn't think it to see me now, and I was confident I could take him. Well, Malcenus was clever and built like a stone tower. Heavy but fast with it, and he used a curved sword like a sica, but longer. Something he'd had made for him in Damascus, and he certainly knew how to use it. I tried to wear him down, then finally had to go in. I managed to get the net over his head and, when he started to move, I thought it was all over. But he fooled me. Instead of falling, he followed the pull of the net and used that sword of his to slash the mesh. I did my best with the trident, but it was like poking a crab with a needle. Then he cut the shaft and I was left with nothing but a shred of net, a stick, and a dagger.'

He fell silent, thinking, remembering, his hand caressing the scar. To him the heat of the room had become the warmth of the sun, the murmur of conversation from those around us the scrape of sandals against sand, the yells coming from the *tepidarium* outside, where someone was having the hairs plucked from his body in the cooler room, became the shouting of the crowd.

A moment I respected and then, as he shuddered, said, 'He got you?'

'He got me.' Arrius was grim. 'He almost cut me in half, and I went down clutching my guts. The crowd was with me, thank the gods, and gave me life.'

The shouts of *ie mittendum est*! Let him live! I have heard it and knew how it felt. To a fighter down and helpless, it was the sweetest sound in the world.

Then, as Arrius moved, wincing, I wondered at the mercy he had been shown. Crippled, he could no longer fight, and gone forever were the days of complacent women and generous men. And only he could know of the pain he'd suffered as his wound slowly healed. How often during that time had he wished that he had been cleanly dispatched with a second blow?

'And Malcenus?' I said. 'What happened to him?'

'He fought for another three years and then retired to Egypt where he lived like a king until someone poisoned him.' Arrius rose, stiffly. 'I've had enough of this. Let's go and cool off.'

Before we entered the *frigidarium* slaves scraped our skins with *strigils*, removing all the oil, dirt, and grease, then, after the cold plunge, we rested on couches while *unctores* massaged us with deft hands.

To Arrius I said, 'What happens now?'

'Where do we go next?'

'Yes.'

He tensed a little and I could guess the reason. As a *lanista* he'd had a bad day, losing two *pugiles* and a Thracian. None had been of high quality, the boxers had been slow, and the Thracian little better than a *tyro*, but their loss had diminished his *familia* and so his potential income.

'I've plans, Atilus,' he said quickly. 'We could head south to Puteoli or Misenum. And I've word of a big *munera* to be held at Tarentum.'

It was even further south and well away from Rome. Once it would have suited me, but I'd had enough of second-rate amphitheatres and cheaply run displays. For almost five years I had moved around, fighting where and when I could, risking my life for small fees and trifling prizes. A necessary precaution at first, but now it was time to change my habits.

'Of course the real money is in Rome,' mused Arrius. 'But what chance would I have against the Imperial Schools? They can turn out all the fighters needed. Cheap slaves used as fast as they are trained. I've got owners to consider, those who have given me charge of their gladiators, and others, freedmen like yourself. But don't worry, Atilus. I'll look after you.'

'I'm not worried. I'm leaving.'

'What!' He reared upright, knocking aside the masseur. 'Leave? You can't!'

'Why not?' I was cold. 'I'm not a slave to be bought and sold. You don't own me.'

'No, but—Atilus! Why?'

The answer was on his face, a blend of greed and anger, a taut desperation coupled with hate. To him I was nothing but a man to be used. Already, perhaps, he had arranged to gain from my end, agreeing with those who were interested in winning high wagers to feed me some compound which would take the edge off my skill, opium or some other insidious drug.

I had seen it happen to others.

In Ferentis a *myrmillo*, popular, heavily backed, had been drugged with the juice of henbane given to him in wine sweetened with honey. He had died on the sand, eyes glazed, mouth gaping, unaware even at the end what had happened to him. In Luceria *cantharidea* had been given to a *cruppellarius* who, crazed by the overdose of potent aphrodisiac, had fallen easy prey to a Thracian despite his heavy, protective cuirass.

'Atilus!' Arrius was pleading. 'Don't leave me like this. At least give me a chance to replace you. One more fight, at least. Just one. Atilus, please, you can grant me that.'

'One fight?'

'Yes. The last. I promise.'

'I know.' I looked at his face, the lines, the greed. 'That's why I'm leaving you, Arrius. The next time I fight, I hope to win.'

Heraculis was waiting and deftly he helped me to dress, nose sniffing as if he were a dog examining a bone.

'No perfume,' he said. 'That's good, master. The rubbish they use in these places is enough to turn a decent man's stomach. We don't want to create the wrong impression, do we?' He squealed as my hand closed around his throat. 'Master!'

'What have you been up to, you worm?'

'Nothing, master, I swear it.' He coughed as I released him, one hand rubbing his scrawny neck. He wasn't hurt and I knew it, but it pleased him to act as if he was. 'I bear a message, that's all.'

'From a man?'

'From a woman, master.' He leered. 'An admirer, shall we say? One of your *amatores*. She waits for you in the *domus* of Cossus Bassius.'

CHAPTER FOUR

It was a large house situated to the north of town and set back some distance from the paved, straight line of the Appian Way. The walls were featureless, plain areas unbroken by windows, marked only by the outlines of a door to either side of which burned torches set in bronze cressets.

I arrived at the end of the first watch as the message had bidden, a delay which had given me time to learn a little about Cossus Bassius. He was a wealthy merchant dealing with the east and importing silk, spices, perfumes, and expensive glassware. A rich man and a cautious one. In the bushes surrounding the house I caught a glimpse of movement and heard the rustle of leaves. Darkness shrouded the area, the pools of light thrown by the torches doing little to relieve the gloom. Framed by them, I was a good target for any bowman, an easy mark for a thrown spear, but who, in this place, would want to take my life?

Even so, I was relieved when the door opened to my knock and a slave ushered me into the atrium where a woman came forward to meet me.

'Atilus!' Her hands reached out to touch my own. 'Welcome to this house. It was gracious of you to accept my invitation.'

I recognised Racilia Rubinia, Bassius' wife, from the description I had been given. She was in her early thirties, a woman of medium height, her figure somewhat full beneath her embroidered stola. Her hair, neatly arranged in a series of tight ringlets, framed her face with auburn curls. Her lips were full, the lower pouting with betraying sensuosity. Her eyes, deep-set, were a sparkling blue. About her hung the aroma of roses.

'Domina.' I bowed as courtesy demanded. 'How may I serve you?'

'Such directness!' Her laughter tinkled as if it were water cascading from a fountain. 'Here I am, a bored and restless woman who has asked you to spend a few hours in her company for the sake of harmless conversation, and immediately you demand to know what I want.'

'I didn't—'

'Put it into as many words, that is true,' she interrupted. 'But the thought was there, as you must admit.'

'How can I deny it?' Smiling, I looked into her eyes as she stood before me, face uplifted. 'And yet, Domina, it would be an honour to serve you in any capacity.'

'A courtier,' she mused. 'I am pleasantly surprised. And a good-looking one at that. Is it true that you come from Britain?'

'Yes.'

'A barbarian and yet you don't look like one.' And then, without a change of tone, she said, 'And were you once a slave owned by Publius Varus Severus?'

I said, tightly, 'You seem to know a great deal about me.'

'More than you think, Atilus. Now, shall we join the others?'

They reclined on couches in the open, inner courtyard, massed lamps casting a soft, yellow illumination over the table, which was heaped with a variety of dishes containing fruit, nuts, small cakes dusted with saffron and coated with honey. As I sat and washed my hands in the bowl proffered by a slave, others came forward carrying salvers piled with succulent dainties: portions of meat and fish, small birds boned and wreathed in pastry, tiny sausages, confections of dried and pounded fruits— a feast to tempt a jaded appetite.

The party was small, two men and a girl aside from Racilia and myself. She introduced me to the others, then sat beside the girl, Emillia. As we ate, slaves kept our goblets filled; they were lithe young men with luminous eyes dusted with kohl, Egyptians probably, and their presence told me much about the master of the house.

Aurelius Licinius gestured one aside as the boy went to pour him wine.

'Welcome, Atilius,' he said casually. 'We saw you fight. That was a neat trick you pulled at the end.'

He was a middle-aged man with a thin, downturned mouth, the creases on his cheeks sharply defined between nose and lips. His toga was of the finest wool and the bracelets on his wrists were of thick gold. His hands, backed by dark, curling hair, were broad, the fingers stubby and bearing several rings, among them that of the equestrian order.

'Leacus was a fool to have permitted it,' said his companion, a younger man, scented, his hair dressed in the Grecian style. 'A fighter should at all times be aware of his vulnerable points. He should be on constant guard against any attack no matter from which quarter it might come. Am I correct, Atilus?'

'That is the theory,' I admitted dryly. 'Sometimes, in practice, it isn't always possible.'

'And yet, surely, if a man could remain calm and detached at all times, it would not be too difficult?' Cadius Publius helped himself to a sliver of fish and ate with the fastidious delicacy of a cat. 'I have an interest in the arena as you may have gathered. It seems to me that, given a particular type of training, it would be possible to turn out a stream of champions. I would appreciate your comments.'

'On what?'

'On the type of training which would produce the result I have described.'

'Cadius, for goodness sake let him eat!' The girl spoke before I could answer. 'He wasn't invited here just to answer your boring questions.'

She had a small, round, almost chinless face which, together with the cosmetics she wore, gave her the appearance of a doll. Like her face, her voice was empty, and I gained the impression that she was an expensive toy, spoiled, cosseted, the daughter of some rich family designed for an advantageous marriage.

Compared to her thin voice, Racilia's tones were the deep, rich notes of a bell.

'You are right, Emillia. Atilus must be starving. Try some of these quails,' she invited, turning towards me. 'They are the speciality of my cook and a favourite of my husband.'

'May I ask where he is, Domina?'

'Away on business—as usual.' Her voice held a casual indifference. 'Some more wine?'

I sipped it slowly as the conversation flowed around the table. Cossos Brassius, I knew, was much older than my hostess, which meant that either he had married late or that she was his second wife. The latter, I guessed, and it had probably been a marriage of convenience. A man in his position would find it profitable to be connected to one of the ancient families, and the woman would have welcomed the merchant's wealth.

A political and commercial union, and it explained the Egyptian slaves. Cossos Bassius must find little pleasure in the patrician he had wed, and she would not care about his association with boys.

I began to wonder why I had been summoned.

At first I thought it had simply been a matter of a frustrated woman wanting a little amusement. There had been many such before, matrons and others who had become sexually stimulated at the sight of blood and who were eager to offer themselves to a successful gladiator. Now, studying Racilia, I felt my first impression had been wrong. Her guests told against it. No matter how corrupt and degenerate Roman society had become, certain rituals were observed. Adultery was not openly flaunted. Lovers, whether slave or free, were rarely publicly acknowledged. A façade, of course, but a pretence which helped to maintain the dignity of those involved. Gossip carried the truth, but custom dictated that such scandal be ignored unless it grew beyond acceptable boundaries.

And how was it that she knew so much about me? It had been years since Publius Verus Severus had sold me to a *lanista*, and the reason why had been kept a close secret. Obviously, Racilia had made some investigations. Or perhaps she had been told. But, if so, by whom?

Aurelius, perhaps? I studied him as I helped myself to fruit. The man was a knight and would be close to the heart of the empire. In the society in which he moved, few secrets remained hidden for long and, even from a hint, deductions could be made. Cadius? I doubted it. He was too young and callow, too concerned in his own needs, and was a type I had met often before.

Now, washing his hands, he said, 'Tell me, Atilus, when you fight, what is your major aim?'

'To win.'

'Of course, but I meant initially. When you first meet your opponent, what do you look for? His stance? I've heard that is important. The way he holds his weapons? That, too, must have significance.' Cadius sipped at his wine and carefully dabbed his lips as he lowered the goblet.

I said, flatly, 'Everything holds significance, but only one thing is essential. The determination to win.'

'An attitude of mind?' He pondered the thought as if it were new to him. 'The killer instinct,' he mused. 'The determination to survive. But that is the attribute of a beast. A man, confronting it, would surely hold the advantage if he maintained control of his calm detachment. A combat is, in a sense, an art. The complex interchange of position and motion which should lead, inevitably, to the final, predetermined blow.'

The man was a fool, spouting theory, talking as if living men were pieces in a game. I had suffered such idiots before and, given patience, I would again in return for the hospitality, but it was never easy.

'Atilus?' Racilia was watching me. 'Your goblet must be empty.' Her voice rose a little. 'More wine for my guest!'

The slave was closer than I knew. Turning, I knocked his arm and spilled a shower of ruby drops over my tunic. Terrified, he backed away, mouth open, strangled noises coming from his throat. Noises, not words, for him they were impossible. The boy had no tongue.

'Atilus! Your tunic!' Racilia rose, her cheeks flushed with anger. She clapped her hands and, as a hulking figure appeared, snapped, 'You! Take that thing away! Beat him until he can no longer stand! Do it immediately!'

Bowing, the major-domo led the shivering wretch away.

Thoughtfully I chewed a grape. A slave, whipped, was nothing, an occupational hazard of his station in life, but if I crossed her, would she remember that I was free? Even if she did, there were many ways in which an offended woman could take her revenge. Assassins could be hired and false accusations made. The word of a gladiator would count for little against that of a patrician.

Mute slaves and guards hidden in the bushes around the house. Both belonged to those engaged in dangerous business, and my unease grew as, rising, Aurelius Licinius cleared his throat.

'An excellent meal, Racilia. Now I think it time we had a little talk. Atilus, I'm sure you will be interested in what I have to show you in the *tablinium*.'

It was a large room normally used for the master of the house to greet his visitors, a place for private conversations and for study. Shelves along the walls were heaped with scrolls and tablets, the records of Cossos Bassius' activities, and a table held a clutter of maps and reports from various agents.

Sweeping them aside, Aurelius settled his bulk on the polished wood. Racilia had accompanied us, leaving Cadius and the girl to their own devices. Faintly I heard the sound of a lyre.

'He plays well,' said Aurelius absently. 'That, at least, should gain him favour with Nero.'

'Which shows the extent to which Rome has fallen,' snapped the woman. 'Actors and musicians in the positions of importance which belong by right to those born to rule. Poets declaiming verse instead of military commanders discussing strategy. Money squandered on effete arts instead of being used to strengthen our frontiers.' Restlessly she moved about the room, touching a phallus carved in ebony and inlaid with mother of pearl, the handle of a riding whip, a statuette of a couple locked in an amorous embrace. Odd things to find in such a room, but I'd guessed that its owner was an odd man.

I said, quietly, 'You were going to show me something?'

'This!' Aurelius thrust his hand into his toga and withdrew it, filled with the weight of a purse. Opening it he spilled a shower of gold on the table. 'A hundred gold pieces, Atilus, and there could be another four. How long would it take you to earn that in the arena?'

In Rome, not long—a man of reputation could claim a high fee for a single combat. In the provinces, the way things were, too long. I remained silent, looking at the gold, conscious of the others and their calculating eyes.

'Take it, Atilus,' urged Racilia. 'It's yours.'

'To compensate for a soiled tunic?'

'As a gift from a friend.' Aurelius was bland. 'Let us call it a delayed appreciation of a service you performed in the past. An errand you ran—and a mouth which you kept closed. Surely you remember?'

An incident five years old now and, yes, I remembered. A journey I had undertaken at night while still a slave to a house in Rome where a woman had waited to give me a certain vial. Locusta, the notorious manufacturer of poisons who had sat like a spider in a web in a house close to the Tiber. And, while I could never prove it, I was convinced that the vial had reached Agrippinilla's hand.

Poison delivered to the mother of Nero, now the Emperor of Rome. A woman consumed by a burning ambition to rule but, being a woman, she could never openly do that; through her son she had power now in fact if not in name. Her husband, the Emperor Claudius, had been an obstacle to be removed. It could have been no coincidence that he had died shortly afterwards, to be deified by the Senate.

Lucius Junius Gallio, the brother of Seneca, Nero's tutor, had made a joke about it based on the custom of public executioners of dragging the bodies of those executed in the prison to the Forum with large hooks, and from there into the river. Lucius had claimed that Claudius had been raised into heaven with a hook, and Nero himself had added to the jest, saying the mushrooms were the food of the gods since Claudius, by eating them, had become a god himself.

Mushrooms poisoned with the stuff I had obtained from Locusta—and now Agrippinilla was sending me gold!

I didn't touch it. Instead I said, my voice slow as if baffled. 'Remember what? I ran no errand for anyone. I was just a fighter, a gladiator-slave.'

'And a discreet one.' Racilia released her breath with a sigh, and I guessed that I had passed a test of some kind. 'But you were more than that, Atilius. For a time you were Nero's bodyguard. Once, at least, you saved his life before he became Emperor.' Her voice changed a little. 'And you know how he rewarded you.'

'He granted me the *rudis* and my freedom.'

'After you'd earned it,' she said quickly. 'Popular demand forced his hand and you know it. He gave you nothing he wouldn't have given to another.'

'But he gave it.'

'Atilus, don't play with us,' she said impatiently. 'Nero is a monster and you know it. Unless he is stopped, he will ruin Rome. He cares nothing for tradition and the sanctity of the past. Just remember what he did to the games. He banned the use of war-captives and even forced senators and knights to fight as if they had been common gladiators. All he thinks about are plays and concerts, dramas and recitals, singing and dancing. Did such things win us what we have? Does watching a play breed a good soldier? Is the strength of Rome to be wasted until we are no better than decadent Greeks? We have a painted fool sitting on Palatine and we must get rid of him before he destroys us all!'

'Racilia!'

Aurelius was startled, not expecting the outburst, but the

colour of her hair should have warned him. The Rubrius were notorious for their short tempers and lack of restraint.

I remembered that Rubria was the eldest of the Vestal Virgins and that Julia, the High Priestess, was an intimate of Agrippinilla, a woman I was certain wished me dead and for fear of whom I had stayed away from Rome.

Now, apparently, she had changed. I was no longer a voice to be stilled but a hand to be used. She, or those involved in her ambition, sought my friendship, and it was easy to guess what would happen should I refuse to give it. Trapped in the house, I could vanish without trace.

On the table the gold shone with a rich, yellow warmth. The stuff which could provide comfort and luxury. Money to buy passage to Greece or Egypt, Syria or Spain. To Britain even, anywhere far enough away from those who had let ambition dull their minds. Money I dared not refuse. Later, when the chance came, I would decide what to do. For now I had no choice.

Aurelius relaxed as I swept up the coins. Racilia, more discerning, said, 'No questions, Atilus?'

'Like these coins, Domina, silence can be golden.'

'No curiosity, then?'

'About what?' Turning I met her eyes, my own bland. 'You have been most generous in regard to my stained tunic, and I appreciate both the meal and your gift. It isn't often that a gladiator's skill is so highly rewarded by a gracious patron.'

I saw her frown at my apparent dullness, then the crease between her eyes vanished as she recognised the opening I offered, the one I prayed she would take. As yet nothing had been said which could harm her or her companions. I could leave, the recipient of a gift, and there would be an end. An end to my involvement with plots and intrigue and the trouble they would bring. And there was a plot, every instinct warned me of it, why else the gold and the mention of things best forgotten?

'You are shrewd, Atilus,' said Racilia. 'But the money was not for your tunic. Neither was it a gift. It is your fee for protecting me on my journey to Rome.'

'Rome?'

'We leave at dawn,' she said. 'Everything has been arranged. You will, naturally, stay here tonight.'

'And my slave?'

'He will be sent for. We shall talk later, Atilus, now let us return to the others. I am sure that Cadius will want to talk about various fighters you have known and the skills they employ.' Racilia smiled, a woman triumphant. 'And I'm sure that we shall enjoy the journey to Rome.'

CHAPTER FIVE

Dawn broke with mist and a scud of rain, both unusual for the time of the year and, to a superstitious man, ominous. The conditions delayed our departure, and the sun was high in the east when we moved north along the Appian Way. Aurelius and Cadius, mounted, rode a little ahead. The women sat in litters borne by stalwart slaves, and from the first it was obvious that my protection was unnecessary.

A dozen armed men marched as escort, tough freedmen with a couple of ex-legionaires among them. Grizzled veterans of the German campaigns who strode along as if they could march forever. The guards who had surrounded the *domus* during the night, I guessed, hard men who wouldn't hesitate in carrying out their orders. And from the way some of them looked at me, I had a good idea of what those orders were.

In effect, I was a prisoner in a cage, the bars of which would remain invisible until I tried to escape.

Heraculis snuffled as he trudged at my side, making much of the burden he carried. It was a light bundle containing a few clothes and little else. The equipment I'd used in the arena had been borrowed from Sentonius. Once I'd owned my own, but bad times had forced me to sell. Now, with gold, I could choose the best.

Early as it was, the road was fairly busy. Carts with solid wheels rumbled towards the town, carrying produce for sale in the market. A file of slaves trotted past, their necks shackled, their overseer busy with his whip. A scatter of pedestrians, some of whom had travelled through the night, risking the danger of brigands.

Despite the police patrolling the road, they were always to be feared. Savage men driven desperate by poverty who were willing to kill for the sake of a few coins. Some were runaway slaves, others deserters from the legions, and all faced the same punishment when caught.

'Master!' Heraculis lifted a hand to shield his eyes. 'Something's going on up there.'

My eyes were better than his and I recognised the figures of uniformed men. As we approached, an officer rode towards us.

'Your name and business?' He nodded respectfully as Aurelius gave the information. 'You have women with you? I thought so.' He glanced at the litters. 'It might be a good idea not to linger.'

'Why not?' Racilia had thrust her head through the curtains. 'What's going on? Are we in danger?'

'No.' The officer masked his scorn with a smile. 'Not with us around to take care of things. It's just that we've caught a brigand and are giving him what he deserves.'

'Then I want to watch!' Emillia swung her legs over the side of her litter. 'Racilia, may I? Cadius, say I can.'

'You can watch,' said Aurelius. 'The slaves also. It will show them what to expect if they disobey.' He sat on his horse, smiling, a Roman watching the might of Roman law. 'Will you be long, officer?'

'No.' The man turned away. 'Hurry with that cross there! Hurry!'

An upright had been set into the dirt at the side of the road, a crosspiece lashed firm some ten feet high. The man the patrol had captured was small, stooped, his face and body bruised and marked with old scars. Naked, the ribs stood out clear against the skin of his chest, and his stomach, shrunken, was a taut expanse between the prominent bones of his hips. He writhed as he was lifted up by soldiers, riding on the shoulders of their companions who laughed and joked as they lashed his wrist to the crosspiece. Another, his face expressionless, hammered a block to the upright beneath the man's feet.

Aurelius said, 'No doubt, officer?'

'None. We caught him almost in the act. A dead man was found a mile down the road and we grabbed this thing as he tried to run into the bushes. He had a purse on him and a silver brooch. A mark on the dead man's cloak showed from where it had been torn. Anyway, he's a branded slave.'

Branded because once he had tried to run, and now, having run again, his fate was sealed. Naked, he hung from his lashings and already his skin was dewed with a patina of pain. It would grow worse as the day progressed and the sun began to scorch his flesh. Thirst would torment him but, above all, he would be racked by fierce cramps in the muscles of shoulders, back, arms, and torso.

A long and dragging death. In order to breathe, the man would have to support his weight on the block at his feet and so ease the constriction of his chest. Sagging, he would begin to asphyxiate and have to support his weight again.

'Are you going to leave him like that?' Emillia's voice was ugly. 'Suppose he has friends to cut him down?'

'It's unlikely that he has,' said the officer. 'But even if he should, they won't get much. You there!' He pointed at a soldier. 'Blind him!'

Two pokes with a spear and it was done. The man screamed as the point found his eyes, ripping into the orbs, sending blood and limpid fluid running down his cheeks. Later the birds would come to peck at the ravaged tissue, tearing the flesh from his lips, his eyes.

He would hang until he died, until he rotted, a grim reminder of the harsh justice of Rome.

'Move!' snapped Aurelius. 'Let's be on our way. I want to reach Bovillae well before dark.'

For a mounted man the journey was nothing. For a man on foot a steady day's walking, but for the litter-bearers it was hard going. Frequent pauses had to be made in order to give them rest.

During one of them Heraculis said, quietly, 'Master, what is happening?'

'Nothing.'

'No?' Like those of a wary animal his eyes were shrewd. 'Men came to me in the night with their orders, and those same men watch every move we make. I may be a slave, master, but I'm not a fool. Patricians don't hire a gladiator for protection when they have their own guards. And a guest isn't watched as if he were a prisoner.'

'You've nothing to worry about.'

'No?' His hand caressed his neck. 'You'll pardon me if I disagree. The last time I was told that my back smarted to the lash. A girl who asked me to do her a favour and, when caught, betrayed me. Be wary of women, master, none can be trusted.' His eyes drifted towards the litters. 'Especially the young one. Such bitches are dangerous.'

He could be right. Yet there was something which could be done.

'Mix among the slaves,' I said softly. 'Find out what you can about the purpose of this journey. Mingle with the guards too, buy them wine if you must, but get them to talk. And be discreet.'

'Always I am that, master, but wine does not come free.' His hand was deft as he took the coins I gave him. 'The veterans would be best,' he decided. 'I've never known a legionaire yet who wouldn't sell his mother for an amphora of wine. But surely you could do better? The woman favours you, I can tell it from her eyes.'

'Just do as I say.'

'To hear is to obey,' he said with false humility. 'Tonight would be best. After we have reached Bovillae.'

We reached it at dusk, passing through the town to a large house beyond. The *domus* was owned by a friend of Aurelius who was absent in Rome, but his steward was expecting us and made us welcome. Wine was provided, food and the use of the baths.

Cadius shared the sunken tub with me. Aurelius was with Racilia, and Emillia, complaining of a headache, had retired early. Impatiently he waved aside the female slave who had come to attend us.

'Women,' he said contemptuously. 'At times I cannot bear the sight of them. Soft, ignorant creatures only good for the bearing of children. We have much to learn from the Greeks, Atilus.'

'Such as?'

'Their sculpture, for example. Have you been to Athens? To Corinth?'

'No.' The water was soothingly warm and I relaxed in it, barely conscious of what my companion was saying.

'I was there two years ago. It was an experience I shall never forget. The temples and palaces put Rome to shame. Poetry expressed in marble and stone. The theatres, the schools, they have to be seen to be believed.' He made a gesture, water dripping from his hand. 'The home of culture.' Again he said, more meaningfully this time, 'We have much to learn from Greece.'

He had, perhaps, already learned too much. I felt the touch of his hand on my thigh, the fingers sliding in an unmistakable caress. They fell as, turning, I rose from the bath and reached for a towel.

'Atilus?'

With an exaggerated yawn I said, 'By the gods, I'm tired. You must excuse me, Cadius, but I need an early night. All that walking—' With a sudden movement I threw him the towel. It hit him in the face. Smiling, I said, 'You were slow. Had we been in the arena, you would now be dead.'

Late that night Racilia came to my room.

I had been given a chamber on the upper floor, a small place equipped with the usual furnishings. A bronze lamp threw a shifting, yellow light, and one wall was decorated with a mosaic of ducks on a pond. I heard the scrape of a fingernail on the door and opened it, thinking that it was Heraculis, hoping that it wasn't Cadius. The scent of perfume and the glow of auburn hair eased my fears.

'Atilus, did I wake you?' She entered the room on naked feet, a robe of diaphanous material wreathing her body. In one hand she held a soft bundle. A tunic made of silk and worth its weight in gold. 'For you,' she said, placing it on the bed. 'In exchange for the one which was stained.'

The one I still wore. Her eyes widened as she noticed that I was fully dressed.

'I was thinking,' I said. 'And must have dozed. I didn't realise it was so late.' Touching the gift, I added, 'You are most kind.'

'To those who serve me well, yes, Atilus. And you are willing to serve me, aren't you?'

'You, Domina?'

She sighed and turned to where wine stood on a table together with an earthenware bowl. Pouring, she sipped and handed it to me.

'Drink, Atilus.' As I obeyed she said, quietly, 'You are a cautious man. I like that. And you have a reputation for being discreet. I like that even more. Nero has reason to remember you and he owes you much. It will be an easy matter for you to get close to him. That can be arranged and, when you are and everything is ready—you understand?'

A stab in the back, a cunning blow to the nape of the neck, poison administered in his wine—yes, I understood. But how was I to escape once the thing was done?

'He is a beast,' she said tightly. 'Insane. Only his mother has been able to control his excesses and protect the welfare of Rome. Yet now her influence is on the wane. Do you realise what that degenerate filth has forced her to do? To sleep with him. To commit incest with her own son. Could anything be more vile?'

'You plot to assassinate the Emperor,' I said harshly. 'And you want me to strike the blow. Woman, are you mad?'

'Were the conspirators mad when they struck down Julius Caesar?' she demanded fiercely. 'They sought only to protect the Republic and killed for the good of Rome. Nero is a beast and must die. The old families must have their privileges restored. There must be an end to the Senate being filled with nonentities and a cleansing of the Rolls. Too many men unfitted for the honour now wear the equestrian ring. Commoners, ex-slaves—'

'Like myself?'

'Some deserve honour,' she said quickly. 'Atilus, co-operate with us and you will rise high. I can promise that you will be granted equestrian rank. A knight, Atilus, think of it! And money too,' she added. 'You will not find us ungenerous.'

'Us?' I saw the shadow veil her eyes and added, quickly, 'You can't be alone in this. And with Nero dead, who will rule? Even if Agrippinilla has the real power, she will have to work through a man. Who will it be?'

A question she didn't answer, but guesses could be made. Aurelius Licinius, perhaps, or someone of his choice. Cadius? I doubted it, and yet it was possible. Whoever it was would have to have the backing of the Praetorian Guard, the strength of their weapons to cow the Senate. Money could buy their loyalty, and Aurelius was rich. And ancient families, jealous of their power, would be willing to back the new Emperor.

'It can be done, Atilus,' said Racilia softly as if reading my thoughts. 'And you are the perfect weapon, which is why I came to find you. As an old friend you will be trusted. As a gladiator you will not be afraid to strike when the time comes. And you have proved your ability to be discreet.'

As she had said, a perfect weapon—and expendable. From what I knew of Agrippinilla, once the thing was done my life would be forfeit. Any woman who could plan the assassination of her own son would not hesitate to murder a freedman. And, if the thing was to be done without her actual consent, she would have reason for vengeance.

Racilia misunderstood my hesitation.

'Money, Atilus,' she said. 'Estates in Gaul or Spain. Equestrian rank and a high official position if you want it. A patrician for a wife and the protection her family can give.'

I said, bluntly, 'You?'

'If you want me, yes.' Her eyes were direct as they looked into my own. 'Cossos will have no choice but to agree to a divorce. And, for me, it will be no hardship.'

Another bribe to add to the rest, and the most tempting of them all. With her for a wife, my future would be assured. As if to give me a taste of what was offered, she stepped a little closer towards me, the scent of her perfume heavy in my nostrils.

'Atilus, kiss me!'

Her lips were soft and yielding, warm with passion, her tongue thrusting against my own. Her hands rose to clasp about my neck and her body, pressed hard against mine, radiated a demanding femininity. A demand which grew as she felt my response.

'Atilus!'

The dancing flame of the lamp threw distorted shadows on the wall as, lifting her, I carried her to the bed.

CHAPTER SIX

It was far into the night when she left and, even when gone, something of her remained, her scent, the memory of her passion, the warmth of her embrace. A woman of fire and determination willing to sacrifice herself to gain her own ends. And yet, there had been nothing counterfeit in her participation. Her need, the declarations of affection, had been not the coin of someone paying for a service, but the genuine emotion of someone on the verge of love.

If I were to kill Nero, she and all that she offered would be mine. To deliver the blow meant little—I had killed before and, with the favour of the gods, would kill again. Yet to kill the Emperor would be to commit suicide and I had no intention of dying.

The chamber held a window facing on the inner courtyard, and I stood at it staring into the night. It held the brooding stillness of approaching dawn, the silence broken only by the distant cries of an owl, the snuffling of dogs kenneled somewhere close. Light showed from a downstairs window, and, across the pale luminescence, I saw the silhouette of a patrolling guard.

A scratch at the door and Heraculis eased himself silently into the room. His leer was suggestive.

'By the gods, master, I think we should change names. I began to think you'd never be alone. Did the woman live up to the reputation of her hair?'

'Watch your mouth!'

'You look drained,' he said, unabashed. 'But I see your efforts were not wasted.' He ran his hand over the silk tunic. 'Keep it up, master, and soon you will be able to change the *gladius* for a toga. The woman could arrange it.' He cringed as my hand closed on his shoulder. 'Master! Please!'

'What have you to report?'

'Little.' He scowled as he rubbed the place I had gripped. 'It is as I suspected, the guards have orders to confine you. Try to leave and—' His hand made a cutting motion across his throat.

'Anything else? Did the woman receive any visitors of note during the past few days? A courier from Rome?' I frowned as he shook his head, the plot then could be in its early stages. 'What about Cadius and the girl?'

'The young man is a certain way inclined, as you may have discovered by now. The girl is a distant connection of the Claudian family. Her father owns large estates in Narbonese Gaul. Cadius Publius is of the Flavian gens and something of a disappointment to his father. He seems to be good at nothing but spending money.' Heraculis sighed. 'Given the chance, I would have been good at that too. Incidentally, master, I have spent all you gave me together with some denarii I had scraped together to provide a few comforts.'

'Liar!'

'The trouble about being owned by an ex-slave,' he said gloomily, 'is that they know all the tricks. But then I have been unfortunate all my life. The gods are against me.' Pausing, he added, seriously, 'As they seem to be against you, master. The ambitions of the high can only cause trouble to such as we.'

'Ambitions?'

'Hints,' he said. 'Just casual talk, but I can smell a plot from across an ocean. Why should Aurelius Licinius make such a man as Cadius his intimate? Certainly not for the love of his body. Slaves listen, master, and not all of them are devoid of tongues.'

'The woman?'

'She has no cause to love the Emperor. Her father was accused of crimes against the state and forced to commit suicide. Her brother has been banished to Spain. Her younger sister caught Nero's eye and, after he had used her, he gave her in marriage to a freedman from Greece.'

Reasons enough for Racilia to hate the Emperor and to join those who wanted him dead. Heraculis grunted as I quenched the lamp.

'Master?'

'Be quiet! Listen!'

I had caught the sound of pounding hooves, a horse hard-ridden and coming towards the house. A porter answered the hammering at the door and the deep voice of Aurelius called a question to be answered by the attendant.

'A messenger from Rome on urgent business.'

'Have him wait in the atrium. Give him wine.'

It was a courier who could be bearing important news. Heraculis caught my arm as I moved towards the door.

Impatiently I snapped, 'Release me. I want to hear what the man has to say.'

'And be caught doing it? There will be guards and slaves in attendance to be sure none overhears.'

'So?'

'Let me do it. I know my way around and have less bulk to hide.'

'And if you are caught?'

'I shall be drunk. The guards can vouch for the amount of wine I have imbibed. You will have me whipped, of course, but I trust you to see that the lash doesn't bite too deep. And,' he added slyly, 'gold is a good remedy for pain.'

'You're a fool, Heraculis.'

'And so are you, master—we have no time to waste.'

He was gone before I could make further protest. Alone I gathered my things in the dark. The silk tunic I bundled beneath my own, holding it with the belt which held my sword and dagger. The gold was already in a belt which I strapped against my skin.

The message could be nothing, but instinct warned me otherwise. Waiting, I strained my ears. From below came the murmur of voices, the touch of metal against stone. Guards moving to seal the *atrium* against intruders, but Aurelius would not talk to the man in the largest room in the house. He would take him to a smaller chamber, one with limited access.

Minutes later Heraculis returned. He was panting a little and, in the dim light coming through the window, I could see that his face was beaded with sweat.

'A slave caught me,' he whispered. 'I had a dagger and used it.'

'You killed him?'

'Before he killed me.' Pausing he said, bluntly, 'Master, Agrippinilla is dead.'

'What!'

'I heard the name twice. The mother of Nero is dead.'

'How? When?'

'The man carried no details, only the news. Aurelius questioned him but could learn nothing more. There were other matters, but the slave discovered me and I had to leave.'

As we should have to leave, and fast. Some wine remained in the flagon and I gave it to Heraculis and, as he drank, looked through the window. With Agrippinilla dead the plotters would be thrown into confusion, but one thing was clear. I had been told too much, and they would be safer if I was dead. Already Aurelius could be moving to see that it was done. And, at any moment, the dead slave could be discovered.

It happened as I watched. From the shadows a man cursed as he stumbled, then his voice rose in a demand for light.

'Murder!' His yell echoed from the walls. 'Turn out the guard! There's an assassin at work!'

Looking upwards I saw the eave of the roof. Heraculis gasped as I gripped him and held him up and out for him to grasp the edge.

'We'll go over the roof and drop on the other side,' I told him. 'Move!'

The roof was of low pitch, covered in baked tiles on which

had grown a crust of lichen. It broke as I gripped it, the sudden loss of traction causing me to slip back to the edge. For a moment I hung, dangling, then as men shouted from below, I heaved myself back to the roof and over it to where Heraculis waited.

'There are men below,' he whispered. 'Two at least. I heard them talking.'

One of them coughed and spat as I listened. His companion muttered something and moved along the building. From the sound of his tread I guessed that he was one of the veterans, a man not easily to be taken by surprise. Crawling to the edge, I looked over, keeping my head low. Dawn was breaking, a nacreous haze illuminating the east and, today, there was no mist.

Below I could see a cleared expanse edged with thick shrubs, all veiled in the soft light which blurred details and gave familiar shapes a distorted aspect. Then, with the clink of accoutrements, a second guard came to join the other who leaned with his back against the wall.

Retreating I pointed towards the corner of the roof and, crablike, we sidled along the slope towards it. As we reached it, a yell came from the room we had left.

'It's empty! He's gone!'

Guards sent by Aurelius to kill me and, now that the alarm had been given, there was no time to waste.

Sliding to the edge of the roof, I swung over it to hang by my hands and, kicking myself outward, let go. I landed with a thud, knees buckling, dirt slamming hard against my back. As I rose a shadow came running towards me, a dim shape holding a lifted spear.

As the point came lancing towards my chest I swayed, knocking it aside with my left arm, the clenched fist of my right slamming hard against the guard's jaw as it came within reach. Hard, but not hard enough. He staggered, shouting, then came at me again, the sword he had torn from its scabbard stabbing towards me in the short, vicious thrust beloved of the legions. My own blade caught it, steel rasping as I swept it up and away, my point lunging at his throat. Habit killed him. His left arm jerked as he tried to lift a shield, but he had no shield, and before he could dodge I'd opened his windpipe.

'Heraculis! Jump!'

I broke his fall as he dropped from the roof, setting him on his feet as men came running towards us. Together we ran from the house into the shrubbery, turning so as to head towards the road. We reached it as horsemen came galloping from the house, some heading towards the town, others towards Rome. They would set up road blocks and enlist the aid of the patrols with a lying story about me having robbed and killed. The dead would provide evidence and Aurelius would claim that I had stolen the tunic and the gold.

'Master!' Heraculis sucked in his breath as he listened to the cautious approach of the men behind us. 'If we follow the road they'll catch us and I'll end on a cross. And if they loose the dogs—' He broke off as a deep baying came from the kennels. 'The hounds! May the gods help us now!'

The gods and speed. In the pale, growing light we were becoming more visible to those who searched for us. A spurt and we had crossed the road and were thrusting our way through the bushes on the far side. For half a mile we ran straight, then I turned to the right where a clump of trees showed against the sky.

'A stream,' panted Heraculis. 'We need water to break our scent.'

Wings would have been better, but to wish for those was to wish for the moon. As the trees closed around us the baying came nearer, the thin shouts of men rising above the belling of the hounds.

'Hurry!' Grabbing the thin wrist I hauled the slave along by brute strength. 'Run, man. Run!'

Two miles at top speed, dodging, taking advantage of every scrap of cover, and he began to flag. Had horsemen been sent after us we would have stood no chance, but Aurelius had sent none, probably relying on the dogs to bring us down. A mistake which I hoped he would regret.

Another mile and rocks showed before us, bare stone which thrust from the soil in a jagged mound. Beyond lay a field crossed with a line of willows footed with osiers and reeds. The natural vegetation of a river or stream.

If we could reach it, we had a chance, but the dogs were too close, their belling too loud. A bad sign, dogs made no noise when on the chase, calling only when they had spotted their prey.

'Get to the willows,' I ordered, pushing Heraculis towards them. 'Get in the water and move west. Hurry!'

'Master—'

'Move!' I drew sword and dagger. 'I'll join you when I can.'

Turning I ran back to the rocks where an outcrop, split, made a crude fortress. Through the gap I looked back the way we had come. If the dogs had been unleashed, they would be well ahead of their masters. Trained to catch runaway slaves, they would leap to grip and hold, to kill at the least resistance.

A slave would have stood no chance, but I was a trained fighter, armed, and man or beast it was all the same.

The first dog fell as my *gladius* split its skull. The second, snarling, howled as the dagger ripped into its throat, jaws snapping as a second blow plunged steel into its heart. The third almost killed me.

It was a savage beast, one of the breed used in the arena, barely tamed and wild with the scent of blood. Rearing, it stood almost as tall as a man, the jaws capable of crunching bone. It came like a missile from a *ballista*, white teeth stark against the ruby cavern of its mouth.

Ducking, I stabbed upwards at the belly, felt the slamming weight of the back legs and went rolling as it landed, blood spouting from a deep gash in its stomach. The wound increased its fury and sent it spinning to lunge at my throat. A stone turned beneath my foot as I rose, throwing me to one side as my left hand with the dagger stabbed upwards, the blade shearing through the lower jaw and burying itself in the upper. As the creature reared backwards, pawing at its mouth, I struck with the sword, the edge driving through fur and bone into the brain beneath.

Jerking free both weapons, I turned towards the gap tense for the next attack. None came. The shouting of men was closer now and I could see running figures in the distance, but there were no more dogs.

The river was wide and deep. It closed around me as I dived, rising to dash water from my eyes. Heraculis waited beneath the overhang of a willow, water up to his chin, his teeth chattering in the chill of the running stream.

'What are you waiting for?' I demanded. 'Can't you swim?'

'Like a fish, master. But where do we head?'

'To the coast. To Ostia. To Rome.'

CHAPTER SEVEN

Rome! The heart of the world. No other city could hope to equal it.

On the hills loomed the bulk of temples and the great houses of the wealthy. The narrow streets were lined with shops and the sprawling mass of Subura sent a continuous susurration of sound through the dusty air. From the Circus Maximus came the roars of those watching the chariot races, a muted thunder which shook the air. Life in the capital was as I remembered it, loud, brash, violent.

Gallus Caecina told me how Agrippinilla had died.

He was a friend, old and wise in the ways of the arena and holding a position to be envied. Once a gladiator, he had become a *lanista*, later joining the Ludus Magnus, one of the Imperial Schools which took men and turned them into gladiators. The Great School to which I had been sold and from which I had gained my freedom.

'Atilus!' He greeted me with genuine warmth. 'Man, it's good to see you!'

'And you, Gallus!'

'You've done well for yourself.' His eyes drifted over my silk tunic, the expensive sandals and the bracelets I wore on my wrists. 'What brings you to Rome?'

'The news.' I met his eyes. 'Agrippinilla is dead at last. Five years is a long time, Gallus.'

'Too long for a good fighter to lose himself in the provinces,' he admitted. 'Not that I can blame you. Well, now you're back where you want to be. Right?'

He smiled at my nod, then turned to look at the courtyard which stretched from the gate where we stood. It was flanked by the buildings which held the various types of gladiators trained in the school, and the open area itself was thick with men hard at work.

Swords flashed in the sunlight as sweating men slammed the heavy practice weapons against posts wrapped in straw, chaff flying, the harsh voices of instructors loud as they yelled commands. Of them all, Primus was the best and I looked at my old trainer as he lifted his voice in a familiar snarl.

'Hit it, man, don't kiss it! That isn't a woman you're facing. It's a man who intends to kill you if given half a chance. Put your back into it. Strike and kill! Strike!'

The lash of his whip emphasised the order, a red weal joining others on the back of the young man wielding the sword.

He hadn't changed. Nothing had changed. I breathed deeply, smelling the familiar odours of the school, the sweat, oil, leather, and grease. To one side a Thracian fighting with the small, round shield and open helmet, using a curved sica instead of a straight gladius, sucked in his breath as a blunted edge sliced across his ribs. Beyond him a laquearius, dressed like a retiarius but using a lasso instead of a net, fumbled his cast and earned a snarling reprimand.

'Fool! Do you want to shame the school? Be as clumsy again and you'll taste hot iron!'

No idle threat, but a burn now might save him from death later. At least it would teach him to put on a good show.

Over wine in a tavern in the nearby Via Labican Gallus told me what had happened to the woman I'd had reason to hate and fear.

'Agrippinilla was riding Nero hard, and he must finally have lost patience. Even so, he invited her to attend the official ceremonies held in honour of Minerva at Baiae. There they had an argument. Nero has taken up with Lollia Poppaea, who is the wife of Otho. His mother didn't like it and said that he was insulting both herself and Octavia, his wife. She insisted that he send Poppaea back to her husband and, when he refused, called both her and Nero things which shouldn't be said in public. I think she was afraid of the woman's influence destroying her own, and she could have been right. Poppaea is an attractive woman. Intelligent too, so they say, and ambitious. A dangerous combination.'

Remembering Racilia, I had to agree. 'And?'

'Nero had ordered a special vessel constructed to his own plans. It was based on those used in the great *naumachia* held by Claudius on the Fucine Lake a few years ago. Were you at the battle?'

'No.' I had missed the naval spectacle, though I had taken part in its sequel.

'They had some ships rigged so that when a part was knocked free the whole vessel would collapse,' said Gallus. 'Nero's was built like it and furnished in the height of luxury. After the quarrel he gave it to Agrippinilla as an act of contrition and suggested that she use it on her return to Antium.'

His cup was empty and I ordered more wine. As he sipped it I said, 'A ship like that must have taken time to build. How was it at the right place at the right time?'

Gallus shrugged. 'Who knows? A whim, perhaps? A coincidence?'

Or the cold-blooded foresight of a cunning murderer. I sat, remembering the young Nero I had known. He had been sixteen then, already engrossed in artistic pursuits; yet a warped and distorted nature had accompanied the undoubted skill. Whims and impulses seemed to govern his life and yet, also, there had been a calculated intent behind many of his apparently spontaneous actions.

'So she drowned,' I said. 'Someone wrecked the vessel when it was in deep water. Well, she deserved it.'

'She didn't drown,' corrected Gallus. 'That woman could swim like an otter.'

He went on to tell me what had happened. Agrippinilla had

been hurt, but she had managed to stay afloat until rescued by a fishing vessel which had taken her to Bauli. From there she had sent word to Nero asking for his help. Instead of aid, he had sent men to kill her.

'She died bravely,' said Gallus. As a Roman he could appreciate that. 'When they broke into her bedchamber, she opened her legs, bared her body and screamed for them to plunge their swords into the womb which had given birth to so monstrous a son.' He added, bleakly, 'They burned her on a pyre made of driftwood. The wife of an Emperor and the mother of another to come to such an end!'

I didn't share his sympathy, remembering the fight when I had won the *rudis*, the extra men she had turned against me in an effort to prevent my survival. I had killed them and would have killed her with a captured trident if Gallus hadn't prevented me.

Watching my face he said, quietly, 'Let the dead rest in peace, Atilus. Five years is a long time.'

'Too long!' It had been five years wasted. Then I'd had my foot on the ladder which had led to fame and wealth. But there was no use regretting the past. Calling for more wine, I said, 'This has to be good for business. Nero will have to ensure his popularity, and how better than to give a series of *munera?* The public are always hungry for entertainment. The Vestals too will demand expiatory games in Agrippinilla's honour.'

'So?'

'I want to take a part, Gallus. It's a chance for me to regain what I lost when that bitch turned against me. I've had enough of the provinces. It's possible that Nero will remember me. One good fight and I could be in his favour.'

Dubiously he said, 'But how? You don't belong to the school now. You have no *lanista*. How about equipment? None? I thought not.' He shook his head, frowning. 'You could always volunteer, but things have been slow, and there are plenty of others who'll be wanting work.'

It was a time to press. I said, 'I'm good, Gallus, and you know it. I'll make an impression and, when I do, you won't regret it.'

Pausing I added, 'And there's a reason why I need to hide in the school.'

I had taken my time reaching Rome, giving the plotters an opportunity to lose their initial panic, but Aurelius Licinius would still have an interest in wanting me dead. Once close to Nero, I would be in a position of strength, but until then I was vulnerable to any hired assassin who could track me down.

For a moment Gallus hesitated then he said, slowly, 'You want to live at the school, eh? Well, it's been done before. You've a slave? Good. That takes care of personal attendance. You'll have to spend a little, but you know about that. And there could be some friction.'

'I'll take care of that.'

'Yes.' A smile lifted the corner of his mouth. 'I imagine you can. A pity I won't be there to see it. Well, let's see what Primus has to say.'

We met him as the men trooped from the exercise grounds and he shook his head, doubtful as he listened to what I wanted.

'We've all the *secutares* we can use. Good men, most of them, and all spoiling to gain a reputation. I'm not decrying you, Atilus, just stating the facts.'

'Give me a net,' I said. 'Set me against your best. I'll show you how good he is.'

Many *retiarii* graduated from the net to the sword, but no swordsman would lower himself to fight as a *retiarius*. It was a matter of pride and prestige, and using the net wasn't easy. It took skill to throw the mesh and handle the trident, but Agonestes had taught me and I had been a willing pupil. Versatility was an asset, but the greatest benefit lay in knowing how an adversary would act, the limitations of his weapons, and how such knowledge could be turned against him.

Now, watched by a scatter of gladiators, I faced a young Gaul who held his sword and shield as he had been taught, who placed his feet just so, and who held his head at the right angle. Allugius had learned well.

He was a slave. A *tyro* yet to have his first real fight. Not the best the school had to offer, but the man Primus had chosen.

'Begin!' he snapped.

I still wore my tunic, feeling remarkably light despite its weight, a feather when compared to my usual equipment. Dancing back as Allugius advanced, I caught his sword on the tines of the trident as I flicked the net at his ankles. He responded well, jerking free his blade as he jumped over the mesh, advancing again with sword and shield at the ready.

Backing I probed, noting the way he moved his sword-arm, the movement of his feet. First the arm and then the feet, never both together. An ingrained habit? He was too much a novice for it to have been a calculated attempt to mislead. His shield was held close, tight against his body, not lifting even when I cast the net. Instead he ducked and weaved and stubbornly refused to retreat.

At any moment now he would make his rush.

It came when I expected it, a burst of energy which sent him flying towards me, sword raised, sunlight glittering on the blade as it swept down towards my head. I caught it on the trident, twisting the shaft so as to trap it between the tines, pushing it up and sideways, so that he was forced to turn and keep turning as I ran in a tight circle.

Then, abruptly, I reversed the direction, stepped close and gripping the shaft with both hands swept up the end in a curve which tore the *gladius* from his hand and sent it flying as the shaft cracked against his wrist. The sword fell a few feet away to land point down in the dirt. Instinctively he ran towards it, stooped to snatch it up and rose to find the net firmly closed over his helmet and upper torso.

A jerk and he was down, my trident poised over his throat.

'Allugius, you're dead,' said Primus disgustedly. 'Act like that in the arena and you'll be jeered. Once down, you wouldn't stand a chance of being granted mercy. Atilus, tell him what he did wrong.'

'You are the instructor, Domine,' I said.

His lips twitched at the title, immediately turning sour as

Allugius climbed to his feet.

'Well? What have you to say for yourself?'

'He tricked me,' panted the man. 'I thought—'

'Just what he wanted you to think,' interrupted Primus, impatiently. 'And of course he tricked you—this isn't a game with delicate rules. You fight to win. Always you fight to win. How you do it doesn't matter. Now listen to me and learn. First you played at the attack and then you came in at the wrong time. Once your sword had been trapped, you should have backed, dodged, done anything to get it clear. And when you lost it— what then?'

'I was helpless. Unarmed.'

'Rubbish!' Primus's anger was searing, matched by his contempt. 'You still had the shield. You could have used it as a hammer, a club, a blunted sword. Well, it proves one thing at least.' He paused for a moment then ended, savagely, 'Double-training for a week and, when you fight, you go in to make up the numbers. I can't risk the reputation of the school on a fool.'

Allugius had no choice but to accept the scorn and fury. To have argued would have earned him the whip. To have vented his rage in physical attack would have condemned him to the cross.

Primus grunted as the man moved away. 'You were good, Atilus, but he was no real opposition.'

'I asked you to pit me against the best.'

'You know I couldn't do that,' he said, flatly. 'To make a fool of a *tiro* is one thing, but the *spectati* are something else. Once a man has fought and won in the arena, he gets a little touchy about being set against a spoiled dilettante.'

'Me?'

'What else are they to think?' he demanded. 'You with that silk tunic and gold bracelets—Atilus, be fair. You look like some rich young fool who wants to try his hand in the arena. We've had a few like that and none has lasted long. One of them was a man condemned by the Emperor for coughing while he sang. Another was found in his stepmother's bed and had to fight in order to gain his father's forgiveness.'

'Did he?'

Primus shrugged. 'I don't know, but I did hear the old man gave him a good funeral. Now to details. We've *secutares* enough, as I told you, but are you willing to be paired?'

To fight as a *provacator*, armed and armoured as a *secutar* but with a different helmet. One open and with a smaller brim. The man I would face would be equipped the same.

'I'm willing.'

'Good.' Primus grunted his satisfaction. 'You'd better move in, but, Atilus, get rid of the tunic and gold before you mix with the others.'

CHAPTER EIGHT

That night I was initiated into the school. Gallus had mentioned the possibility of friction and I had expected it, in doubt only as to the direction from which it would come. Oratius was the instigator.

He was a *myrmillo*, built like a gnarled tree, his arms as thick as an ordinary man's thighs. His shoulders and upper back were ugly with scars, more puckered tissue on his legs, a livid scar on the angle of his jaw. *Myrmillones* fought with open helmets, a heavier shield than that used by a *secutar*, and with a band of metal protecting stomach and lower torso. Big, burly men, they depended on brawn rather than brain. Now he sneered at me as we stood in the hall where the gladiators spent their time between the evening meal and being ushered to the rooms where they slept.

'A pretty-boy,' he said. 'A delicate flower from some fine household. What happened, Atilus, did you put your hand up the wrong skirt?'

'Don't talk to him like that, Oratius,' called another. 'You'll hurt his feelings.'

'I'd like to hurt something.' Allugius, smarting from his defeat, scowled with anger. 'I'd like to open up his guts with a sword.'

'And spoil his sensitive skin?' someone grinned with a flash of teeth. 'If you did that, what would his mother say?'

'His lover, maybe. Hey, perhaps that's why he's here. He wants to be among men!' The speaker, a Thracian, shoved himself forward in the circle around me. 'Is that what it is, Atilus?'

I said, coldly, 'Shut your mouth!'

'You want to shut it for me?' He grinned with anticipation. 'I'm ready if you are.'

Behind me someone rattled a pot on the table and a spray of droplets fell over my head from a flung handful of water. A voice called a suggestion.

'How about making him run the gauntlet?'

'That's an idea.' The Thracian facing me welcomed the suggestion. 'Get ready, boys and we'll make him jump!'

'Off with his tunic and let's see how fast he can move!'

Horseplay I had expected and a little I would tolerate, but there were limits, and to run the gauntlet was to risk being crippled or blinded. The men wouldn't be gentle and already some were arming themselves with heavy straps and staves. Stripped, I would be forced to run between them and be beaten as I ran. An experience common to all novice gladiators as a test of their mettle, and one I had known. One I had no intention of repeating.

Thrusting aside the Thracian, Oratius came towards me, one hand reaching for the tunic of coarse wool I had changed for the one of silk. As his fingers touched the fabric I spat in his eyes.

As he reared back, blinking, I struck at his throat, missed the windpipe, but caught him on the side of the neck. It was like hitting a wall. I struck again as he lifted his hands, bringing blood from his nose before ducking beneath his blow. Wind stirred my hair and I struck again, this time low to the belly. Roaring, he followed me as I backed, his fists beating the air. Against a *pugile* I would have stood little chance, but Oratius was accustomed to using sword and shield, and used his clenched hands as if they had been hammers. My own speed worked to save me, but I took a punch on the shoulder and another to the side of the head, which caused my senses to swim. Then the edge of the table hit against my spine.

'Now!' yelled a man. 'Get him, Oratius! Knock him flat and we'll have him stripped and running before he knows it!'

Crowded around the bulky figure, the others gave me no opportunity to dodge. With my back hard against the table I was unable to retreat. For a moment I blocked his blows as if facing a swordsman and then, as he came in for the finish, I threw myself backwards over the table, lifting my legs to roll over it and to stand upright on the other side. A hand caught my tunic and ripped it from my shoulders, so that I was almost naked when I recovered my balance. An earthenware pitcher stood in a puddle of slopped water and I snatched at it, lifting it high as the *mymillo* lunged over the table towards me, slamming it down hard on his cropped head.

It burst like an egg, spilling water over the man's face and thinning the blood which ran from his nose. As he stood dazed, I grabbed him by the neck and held a shattered fragment of pottery an inch from his right eye.

Harshly I said, 'Give up or I'll blind you!'

The jagged point threatened his pupil; a thrust and it would rip the delicate tissue and leave the eye an oozing ruin.

'By the gods, he means it!' said a man. 'Look at his face!'

My face had become a tiger's mask, the scar livid on the left cheek. And the man was right, I did mean it. What had started as a little rough fun had gone too far. Pride would force Oratius to master me, but that same pride would cost him an eye and maybe his life if he stubbornly refused to admit defeat.

Another voice saved him.

'Look at his back! That scar! I know a sword-cut when I see one. Atilus is no spoiled darling. Oratius, you've caught yourself a fighter.'

He said, thickly, 'A gladiator?'

'One of the best.' A man at the edge of the crowd spoke for the first time. He was grinning, his head held at an odd angle, a scar livid at the side of his neck. A slave-gladiator who had been spared and who now performed menial work at the school. 'I've been waiting for this,' he chuckled. 'I remember Atilus from the old days. He won the *rudis*.'

It was enough, there could be no shame in yielding to a man

who had proved his worth in the arena. I felt Oratius relax and stepped back, dropping the shard. Ruefully he wiped his nose with the back of his hand and stared at the blood.

'Massa, you should have told us.'

'And spoilt the fun?' The man shook his head. 'I've not enjoyed myself so much for years. I like to see a good fight.'

He and the others; but the danger was past and now, accepted, and I could afford to relax. My popularity increased when I bribed an amiable guard to fetch wine and, like a stone thrown into water, I became one with the anonymity of the school.

It was a hard life for hard men. The bulk of gladiators were slaves, usually war captives, condemned to the arena. They were trained for two years and would have to fight for three when they then continued as Massa had done, working until they died. For them the only hope was to win the *rudis* and buy themselves free with the gold they could later earn. A freedom which usually meant they changed their status, not their profession. Many freedmen, like myself, continued to fight from choice. But they were few, as were the survivors of three years of fighting. Aside from the few shown mercy, half of all contestants died during each *munera* and, with others succumbing to wounds, the turnover was high—which accounted for the fact that no one at the school aside from the officials and a few old slaves remembered me.

Not all gladiators were slaves. Many were free men, some even Roman citizens who for various crimes had been sentenced to the arena. They too would train for two years and fight for three, but then were free to go their own way. Among them were volunteers, ruined and desperate men who hoped to make their fortunes, others who had deliberately chosen the arena as their career. Some lived, the majority died, but all had to take the grim oath of obedience, the penalty of breaking which was to be burned, chained, whipped, and executed.

Aroused at dawn, we exercised until dusk and Primus saw that I received no privileges. For hours at a stretch I hacked at the straw-wrapped posts using each arm in turn. Swinging weights had to be dodged, with ugly bruises the reward for slowness. With ankles held in a short hobble, wrists lashed behind me, I had to dodge the stinging lash of supple wands. Loaded with overweight armour I ran endlessly around the exercise ground. Every weapon used was twice its normal weight.

At times I thought of Cadius Publius and his theories how a gladiator should be trained. Here, in the Great School, as in all the other gladiatorial schools, they knew of only one way. To instruct, to demand constant effort, to use whips and hot irons and a rigid discipline to turn slaves into men determined to kill.

The days slid past and I became reaccustomed to the masses of barley served at every meal. We gladiators ate a great deal of it, believing that it thickened arteries and slowed bleeding, which was the reason we were known as *hordearii* or barley eaters. I had my doubts as to its effectiveness, as I had reservations as to the special ash fed to us after exercise. Only the physicians who prepared the compound knew exactly what it contained, but I guessed that certain vital organs of men and beasts were mixed with herbs and selected plants, the whole burned to concentrate the essences. Dutifully I swallowed the gritty mess. As I had chosen to be treated the same as the others, I had no choice and perhaps it did increase vitality and numb the sensitivity to pain.

A month after joining the school I had a visitor. Gallus Gaecina announced her, looming in the darkness beyond my door. It was well into the second watch, and the school was wrapped in shadow only the patrolling guards awake.

'Atilus, there's someone to see you. A woman.'

'Alone?'

'Her escort is waiting outside.' In the lamplight streaming through the open door his face was anxious. 'You don't have to see her. A way can be found if you want to vanish.'

A choice—and looking at the man I was grateful. He guessed more than I'd told and had suspicions he'd never voiced, but if I ran now my chance at fame would be lost.

'I'll see her, Gallus.'

She was dressed in a sombre robe, a thick veil masking her

features, but the auburn hair glimmering in the light as she lifted her veil was unmistakable as was her voice.

'Atilus.' Racilia Rubrinia extended her hands.

'Domina.' Gently I touched them. 'This is a welcome surprise.'

'Is it?' She searched my face with her eyes. 'Atilus, I have to know. What do you intend?'

'To fight before the Emperor. To catch his attention and, I hope, to gain his favour.'

'And?'

'To retain the regard of old friends. People who were generous to me and one in particular who was more than kind. I would not like her to have misgivings about words spoken in idle conversation.' She relaxed a little, some of the tension draining from her face, yet still mistrust remained in her eyes.

'How did you find me?'

'A guess, Atilus. After you left so abruptly I thought it possible that you had made for Rome. Cadius made some discreet enquiries and here I am.'

'An adornment to my humble chamber.'

'Where you live alone?' She glanced at the two cots. 'No girl to ease your nights?'

'No.'

"And no roommate? No *colluser?*"

'My servant uses the other bed,' I added, after a moment. 'He will not intrude.'

'So.... You look well, Atilus.'

'You also, Domina, and let us hope that we both remain healthy. Of course,' I added, pointedly, 'if for some reason I should be found dead, stabbed, or poisoned, for example, then your own future could be in danger. A dead man poses a mystery as to how and why he was killed. Questions could be asked and, perhaps, answers found. The Emperor, I understand, is sensitive on certain matters. I am sure you understand what I mean.'

Only a fool would not, and she was far from being a fool. It would be a natural precaution for me to have lodged information about the plot with a friend and, to Nero, a hint would be enough. I had given her no choice but to trust me or take the risk that I had lied. A risk, I hoped, she would be reluctant to take.

'You are shrewd, Atilus,' she said after a silence. 'It was clever of you to come here. Walls and guards used to keep slaves confined also serve to keep others out. Do we then forget the past?'

'Not all of it, Domina.' She was a woman, and one with a spirit which would put many men to shame. A patrician whom it would be an asset to have as a friend. Quietly I added, 'Some things are impossible to forget.'

'The dogs?' She chose to misunderstand me. 'That was a mistake and none of my doing. Aurelius loosed them before I could stop him.'

'I was not thinking about the dogs.'

'What then?' A flush touched her cheeks. 'It is best that some things are not remembered.'

The shame of having offered me her body and the promise that she would become my wife. She would have found that hard, even though others of her rank had not hesitated to find pleasure in the arms of a gladiator.

To change the subject I said, 'Where is Aurelius Licinius now?'

'On his way to Egypt. He had matters demanding his attention.' Her voice was bitter.

'Send word after him and tell him that he has nothing to fear,' I said. 'That is, of course, unless I should be found dead. If men are looking for me, call them off. What about Cadius and the girl?'

'Neither knew what was intended.'

'And your collaborator in the Praetorians?' I shrugged at her expression. 'It is obvious that you had to have one. Well, calm his fears also, and take some advice, Racilia. Stay well away from plots and those who hope to use you. Live and be happy.'

'Happy? After what Nero has done? He—'

'Banished your brother, used your sister, and caused the

death of your father,' I interrupted impatiently. 'But is your sister happy? If not, an assassin can rid her of her unwanted husband. Your brother can be recalled to Rome if you work on his behalf. Your father—well, all men die at one time or another. And those who sit at the centre of power must expect to be hurt at times.'

'By a beast?'

'Is any man anything else at times? You have toyed with the idea of killing Nero. Why not influence him instead? Laugh at his jokes, praise his songs, take an interest in his plays and music. Get him to recall your brother from banishment. Use him and gain what can be gained. Don't try to destroy yourself with hate.'

For a moment she looked at me then, turning, sat on the edge of one of the beds. As she settled, the robe parted and I could see the stola beneath, the embroidered fabric taut over the swell of her breasts.

'Atilus, why are you telling me this?'

'Beauty is fragile and too easily destroyed. You own a beauty given by the gods, but they also gave you a mind. Use it in order to stay alive.'

'Is life so important?'

She spoke with the detachment of her class, the near-disdain which filled me with a sudden anger. To a Roman death was nothing when it came to another. Suicide, a favour granted so as to conserve family wealth by the Emperor when he saw fit, or a way taken by those condemned to escape trial, was accounted a deed of honour. Staring at her face in the lamplight I saw, not the smooth patrician features, but a visage tormented with fear of imminent destruction. A fancy born of the dancing flame and one rooted in memory.

'Life, Domina?' My gesture took in the school, the men sleeping in their rooms. 'Ask those who must fight to retain it what value it has? They have nothing else and, to keep it, they must rob another. Think of what it means. Imagine how it feels. Each time they fight could be the last.'

'Atilus—'

'What else can be more important than life?' I ignored her interruption. 'Without it there is nothing. Nothing! Think, woman, of the pleasures you have known. The caress of a loving hand, the food, the wine, the touch of soft garments. Smell the air when you walk and listen to the songs of birds, the laughter of children. Watch an animal with its young. Play with a baby or child. A child—'

I broke off, feeling acid in my throat, the fury of anger begin to engulf me. She who had so much to belittle the only asset of those who had nothing!

'Atilus!' My anger had frightened her. Now she rose, gripping the robe tightly about her. 'Your face! Please!'

Breathing deeply I said, 'Have a child, woman. Then you would think more highly of the life you pretend to despise.'

'I can't! I—' She swallowed, then her face became rigid as if she wore a mask of stone. 'The gods have cursed me,' she said bleakly. 'I am barren.'

'Then adopt one. Would your husband object?'

'Perhaps not, but his interests are not mine. And it is not in my nature to turn my back on the world when there is so much to be done.' She stepped towards the door with a rustle of garments. 'You have confused me. It is time that I left.'

I made no effort to detain her. 'And?'

'I will think about what you have said.' As she reached the panel, she turned to face me and I could see the liquid glinting of her eyes. 'Nero will shortly be in Rome and I will do my best to make my peace with him. It will be hard, but I will do it. Julius belongs in Rome, and if the Emperor's favour can end his banishment then I will gain it. That advice at least I will follow.'

Her brother would gain from her sacrifice, but I wanted more.

'And we are friends?'

'More than friends.' Impulsively she stepped towards me and rested her hand on my arm. Her fingers were slender but they gripped with a surprising strength. 'I will do what I can to help you. I owe you that. And, Atilus, you are right—some things can never be forgotten.'

CHAPTER NINE

Eager to enhance his popularity, Nero spared no expense. The games thrown to honour his dead mother were to be the finest spectacle Rome had ever seen, and for days before the event heralds announced the coming attractions. They were held in the Circus Maximus—no other amphitheatre would be large enough—and long before dawn everyone who could obtain one of the coveted seat-tokens had thronged into the stands.

Lubius Vinius Hormus, the Master of Games, had done his best to satisfy all tastes. The condemned prisoners used as *trinqui* were dressed in appropriate costume and made a part of various scenes. These sacrificial victims used as an offering to the gods had no hope of victory or reprieve. Some, dressed in skins to emulate Hercules, were sent against lions and bears. Others, poorly armed and in many cases bare-handed, faced tigers, wild dogs, boars, bulls, and elephants. Girls were spread-eagled on low couches and ravished by jackasses; and others, daubed with the exudations of female apes, were victims to the lust of chimpanzees.

Bestiarii followed the victims into the arena, killing the animals with sword or spear. Some, mounted, used lances and bows in a bloody carnage which appealed to the blood-lust of the spectators and their inherent savagery. A savagery which chafed at the dances and music, the plays and the singing which Nero held in high regard, and which Hormus used to ease the tension and provide a change from the more popular events.

But one unusual incident appealed to the humour of the

crowd.

Simon the Magician had come from Chaldea claiming to own mystic powers and for a time had been well-regarded by the Emperor. Events had turned against him and, in an effort to regain his influence, he had asked to be allowed to demonstrate his ability to fly.

I watched with interest as he made the attempt.

Sailors had set up a high mast in the arena, guyed and with a small platform at the summit. Wooden crosspieces nailed to the pole provided a means of reaching the top. Simon was a lean, swarthy man with deep-set, burning eyes. He wore a garment adorned with astrological signs, and to each arm he had fastened a wing of gilded feathers.

Heraculis grunted as, awkwardly, he began to climb.

'The man's a fool, master. He has to be. No man can fly, and it is an affront to the gods to even attempt it. Had they wanted us to emulate birds, they would have given us wings.'

Mad or not, Simon was obviously sincere. Before coming to Rome he had joined the Christians, offering their leaders a high price if they would teach him the secret of raising the dead, which rumour claimed they possessed. A useful thing if it could be learned. Good gladiators were expensive, and any *lanista* would pay well if one could be restored to life after he had been killed.

Disenchanted with the Christians, Simon had sold his lesser skills: telling fortunes, finding stolen jewellery, reading the stars, and interpreting dreams. He had sold love philtres also, together with aphodisiacs and compounds to induce miscarriages. Now he intended to fly.

Perched on the summit of the mast he looked very small. The sun caught his gilded wings and turned them into a blaze of lambent gold. For a moment he stood with them outstretched then, abruptly, launched himself into the air. For a moment he seemed to hang motionless and then, as the crowd caught its breath, he fell like a stone to land on the sand before where Nero sat, his blood spattering the marble podium.

'As I told you, master,' said Heraculis scornfully above the roar of laughter from the watchers. 'The man was mad.'

The sound of *tubae* announced the end of the episode and, as the trumpets stilled, the gladiators began their march.

As always we made a brave spectacle. By custom we wore the armour of the original Samnites: crested helmets adorned with brightly coloured plumes, heavy shields embossed with elaborate designs, cuirasses and greaves shaped to fit the flesh they covered, and every scrap of metal was polished to a brilliant finish. Our cloaks were of all colours of the rainbow, heavy with gold and silver thread. Behind us came slaves bearing the actual equipment in which we would fight.

Halting before the Emperor, we lifted our arms and roared the traditional salute.

'Ave, Imerpator, morituri te salutant!'

Greetings to Caesar from men about to die. The last time many of us would give it. A salute which he acknowledged with a casual wave of his hand. If he saw me or recognised me, he gave no sign, turning to the woman at his side and offering her a sweetmeat from a bowl.

Nero had changed since I'd last seen him. Younger than myself, dissipation had softened his cheeks and fleshed his bones, so that he looked rotund beneath his silken garments. The hair which he had trained to fall over his eyes was a distinctive red. His lips were full, the lower sensuous and slightly pouted, giving him an air of femininity. An impression heightened by the way he moved his hands, the touches of paint on his eyelids and cheeks.

The woman at his side was Lollia Poppaea, and about her rumour had not lied. Older than Nero, she looked younger, the stola of silk hugging the full contours of her body. Pearls encrusted it and more rode in the mass of ringletted hair. Her face was round with wide-set eyes, and her chin betrayed a firm determination.

A woman, I guessed, who would rule with a native guile, hinting rather than ordering, receiving gifts with a gushing incredulity which would make the giver yearn to offer more. No wonder Agrippinilla had hated and feared her. She, a woman, had recognised the danger of her own kind.

Back in the preparation rooms beneath the stands Heraculis helped me to get ready.

The ornate armour was set aside and the other was fitted piece by piece. I took trouble over the straps and made sure the belt was tight. All that remained was to don the helmet and to take up sword and shield.

Leaving Heraculis, I moved through the throng, snarling impatiently as a man blocked my passage. A crowd was normal at such times; gladiators, their personal slaves, others from the schools, more from the amphitheatre itself, together with a mass of attendants and officials, but the man was none of these. He was a degenerate who found a sick pleasure in fondling the bodies of the hapless prisoners as they were led to slaughter. Now he hung around the gladiators, knowing that many of them would soon be dead.

He fell aside to the thrust of my arm and I moved on to where a row of images were set against a wall with burning braziers standing before them. Taking incense from a box I made sacrifice to Mars, Hercules, and Nemesis. The stuff burned well, wreathing the stained carvings with smoke.

'A good omen,' said a familiar voice behind me. 'Atilus, can it be you?'

'Agonestes!' Our hands rose to rest on each others shoulders. It was good to see him. A Greek with Greek ways, I had last seen him five years ago when he had only days left to finish his sentence at the school. Of all the gladiators, he had been closest to me and, always, I had feared we would be paired to fight. Now, frowning, I looked at his near-naked body, the net which he held over his arm. 'You must be crazy. You don't have to fight. You were freed when you'd served your time.'

'A man must eat, Atilus.'

'But you had a rich patron.'

'Paccius grew tired of my body,' he said flatly. 'And to be

truthful, the sight of him had begun to turn my stomach. There were others, of course, but a man needs to advertise. And I'm not as young as I was.'

Young or not, and he was ten years older than myself, Agonestes was the best *retiarius* I had known. His lithe body, a heritage from his Greek forebears, was unscarred aside from a thin cicatrice high on his right thigh. A man whom many women would desire, but one whose affections were reserved for those of his own sex.

He frowned at the sound of the trumpets.

'I must get into position, Atilus. If I live, we'll drink wine together later. It is agreed?'

'If I live, Agonestes, yes.'

The qualification which had to be made by any gladiator due to fight.

And the real fighting was due to begin.

Paegniarii had occupied the crowd, cripples and old men fighting mock battles with whips and staves, comic turns to pave the way for what was to come. Now, the *prolusiones* over, there would be real weapons, the display of blood and pain for which the spectators crowded in to the stands waited.

I heard them roar as a score of *retiarii* together with as many *secutares* ran into the arena. Trainers followed them accompanied by slaves bearing heavy leather straps, which they would use to lash the reluctant into battle. Within minutes the sand was dotted with weaving fighters, the shouts of the crowd swelling like the roar of surf as one after the other fell to face the downward jerk of thumbs.

Agonestes smiled as he passed me. An easy victor, he was untouched, a sheen of sweat covering his body, flecks of blood dotting his arm and legs, crimson which had splashed from the wounds his trident had given.

We had no time for conversation. Others not so fortunate came limping over the sand. Two had deep cuts on the legs and arms, a winning *secutar* pressed one hand to his stomach, the bulge of intestines showing through his fingers; another still had a trident dragging from his flesh.

Quickly slaves bustled the hurt into the inner room where physicians waited to tend their injuries. It was a dank place, dimly lit, with couches and tubs of water waiting together with piled bandages. Braziers held searing irons, and strong slaves held the injured as the physicians cut and cleansed and burned. There would be wine, also, heavily laced with opium to help deaden the pain. And, for those too badly hurt, a hammer which would crush their skulls and give relief.

'Atilus?' An official called my name as he pushed through the cluster at the portal. 'Atilus?'

'Here!'

'Good. You're on next. Better get ready, the *tubae* will sound at any moment.' He was plump, puffing, his face glistening with sweat. His tunic was soiled and dirt stained one arm. 'There's been a change. It's to be a fight to the last survivor.'

'A melee?'

'No. Diminishing pairs. Now hurry and take your place.'

He was too concerned. On the sand slaves were still busy raking the patches of blood, while acrobats jumped and tumbled with an easy grace, but performances were run with careful timing.

Heraculis came towards me bearing my sword and shield, the helmet perched on his head. Wrapping a strip of linen about my forehead I donned the helmet. The fabric made it fit snugly, and would also help to keep perspiration from falling into my eyes. The shield fitted I reached for the sword.

Handing it to me, Heraculis said, 'Master, this is bad news. Only one to survive.'

'You doubt my chances?'

'I'd be a fool if I didn't,' he said frankly. 'And if you should fall—what happens to me?'

'That's your worry.' Then, as his face betrayed his concern, I added, 'Don't be afraid. I've made the arrangements, and Gallus Caecina has my will. If I should fall, you'll be freed.'

The roar of the trumpets drowned any reply he might have

made, and a whip cracked somewhere to spur on a laggard contender. In a neat line we ran from the portal to take up places on the sand.

Nero had ordered the alteration. Instead of pairs fighting and the victor going free to fight another day, the survivors of the first bout would be paired to fight again immediately, and so on until only one man was left.

A rare novelty and one appreciated by the crowd. Gladiators were too costly to be normally used in such a fashion, and untrained slaves lacked the skill to be entertaining. They would be cheap but their performance would be poor. As it was, the betting would be intense, the odds high, and a shrewd or lucky man could end the day rich.

And the lone survivor would be famous.

He would also have to be good.

There were thirty-two of us, sixteen pairs, which meant the winner would have to fight and win five times in succession. A demanding performance to ask of any man faced, as he would be, by trained fighters as determined as himself.

My only chance was to get in fast, kill quickly, and conserve my energy. To use every scrap of skill I had gained and to use every trick in the book.

Marshals positioned us and again the trumpets sounded. As they fell silent the battle commenced.

My opponent was young, unscarred, which meant that he was either new to the arena or remarkably skillful. I decided on the former and was proved right. As he backed I moved in, feinted with my sword, caught his *gladius* on the edge of my shield, swept it up and away and, before he could recover, had lunged, my blade striking up and into the exposed armpit, blood spurting as I twisted the sword before jerking it free.

He stared at me, shocked, not realising that he was as good as dead. A second cut and he was down, the jeers of the crowd accompanying the derisive jab of their thumbs.

Casually Nero gave the signal to kill.

I made it quick and painless, my sword slicing into his throat and severing the great arteries. As a man dressed as Charon came running over the sand, another wearing the apparel of Mercury following, I looked around. Two others were already down, three were staggering, wounded but stubborn, others fought with every ounce of energy they possessed.

I noted them; later they would be slow and tired, and their early expenditure of energy would tell against them.

The charonian grunted as he examined my fallen opponent, then signalled to his helpers. With the speed of long practice they dragged the body with the aid of hooks and ropes to the Porta Libidiensis, the Gate of Death. Moving to another of the fallen, the charonian tore off his helmet and with a short hammer he took from his belt smashed in the temple, lifting the tool for all to see the brains and blood smeared on the head.

My second opponent had been wounded, a cut on his left shoulder hampering the movement of his shield. Beneath the helmet his face was taut with strain, his eyes bloodshot. A Spaniard who had been full of confidence in the school but who had lost it on the sand. A man who had forgotten all he had learned in previous fights.

Again I went in fast, slamming my shield against his body, using it as a barrier against his blade as I struck again and again at his wounded shoulder. His shield rose higher each time as I knew it would, metal clanging as my edge bit into the upper rim. Three times and then I dropped to my right knee, the *gladius* cutting at the exposed portion of his leg above the greave. A deep, dragging cut which sent the notched edge grating on bone, possible only because of his careless handling of his shield.

As blood spurted from the lacerated flesh I rose, backing, circling to force him to turn, to put his weight on the crippled limb. Normally I would have played to the crowd, stretching the encounter, letting the loss of blood do its work and, by pretence, giving him a chance to gain mercy. But now there was no time for that. The sun was too hot, the exertion too strenuous. When next I attacked he was off balance, his sword clashing on my helmet, my own darting over the rim of his shield, the point reaching an eye, penetrating the ball to bury itself in the brain beneath.

Two down and now the crowd was yelling my name.

'Atilus! Atilus! Atilus!'

A group of plebeians in the upper tiers of the stands who waved fans and scraps of cloth, screaming as they rose to cheer my victory. Racilia's work, perhaps, the men and women bribed to shout and give their support. But with their voices came others from the lower tiers and even from the podium on which high dignitaries sat in marble chairs softened with cushions.

'Get them, Atilus! Cut out their guts! Kill! Kill!'

The third man was a veteran, an old hand and a first-class fighter. Like me he was unwounded, his breathing regular, his very stance betraying his confidence.

He even wasted his breath in talk.

'A deal, Atilus. A quick end for the one who goes down.'

'Agreed.'

'I've no wish to be a cripple and no charonian is going to smash in my skull. So a clean fight and no tricks, right?'

'Right.'

He must have thought me a *tiro*.

I maintained the illusion, backing, my head turning, breathing faster than I had need. Confidently he came in, shield held protectively before him, sword glimmering in the sun as he stabbed at my face. A feint, but I reacted as he expected, my shield lifting to block my face. A moment only, but enough to fix the pattern of my defence in his mind. Twice more I did the same, making sure each time that I was at a safe distance, continuing to back as he pressed forward.

Now, from the crowd which had cheered me, came jeers.

'He's turned soft, Noblior!'

'Make for his eyes!'

'Ten gold pieces for what he carries between his legs!'

The last came from a woman. A good wife and mother perhaps who had allowed emotion to overcome her. I ignored them all, the shouts and the jeers, watching, concentrating on the man who intended to kill me.

One who thought I was already as good as dead.

I could tell it by his face, the assurance which gleamed in his eyes. No tricks, he had said, and I had agreed, but only a fool would have thought we meant what we said. So when his sandal dug at the sand to kick a mass of flying grains towards my eyes, I was ready. The sand hit my shield and, as he rushed forward, I sprang in turn to pass him close on his left side, shields grating, my sword lifting to fall in a slashing cut to his exposed back.

A blow which sent the point deep, dragging over the spine as I snatched back the blade, a gush of blood following the steel.

'Atilus!' The shout from the crowd was a scream. 'Atilus! *Verbera! Verbera!*'

Strike! Strike! Show us blood, the gleam of bone, the red muscle beneath the skin. Give us another's pain. Give us spectacle. Give us butchery.

The cry, the madness, the mania of Rome!

Noblior was wounded but far from dead. He spun, snarling, his blade slicing air as I dropped and slashed at his thighs. One cut and then I was thrusting, the blade pointed upwards, the point rising beneath his kirtle to plunge deeply between his legs.

Blood spattered my hand and arm as I twisted, then jerked free the blade. Noblior screamed like a stricken beast and fell, vomiting, not seeing the sword I lifted, the blow which took his life.

Panting, I looked around. The sand was spattered with blood, ridged with the thrust of sandals, long furrows leading to the Gate of Death. To one side a gladiator looked at the fallen body of his opponent and then, as I watched, fell to twitch feebly, too weak from his wounds to stand. Another clutched the stump of his left arm from which spurted ruby streams.

Only one man other than myself remained on his feet in any condition to fight.

A man who was lucky or clever. Younger than Noblior, his body scarred, his eyes elongated and gleaming like topaz beneath the rim of his helmet.

Dropping my sword I knelt and rubbed the blood from my hand, catching up the blade as officials urged us to stand before the Emperor. I saw his eyes widen a little as he looked at me, then his hand lifted, hung poised for a moment, then dropped.

The crowd fell silent. A tense hush replaced the earlier noise as eyes strained and bodies reared from their seats. A fortune waited for those who had backed the victor—who would it be?

And then, as our blades touched, a woman unable to bear the tension screamed, 'Kill him, Scaeva! My body is yours if he dies!'

Other voices joined that of the woman, yelling promises, encouragement, urging us both to kill. And then, again, the hush descended.

A brooding stillness in which small sounds were magnified; a cough, the rustle of a garment, the thin, harsh ringing of our swords.

Scaeva was lithe, fast on his feet, a killer with a brain. I watched his arm, his eyes, the movements of his eyes. A slight withdrawal of his shield preceded a thrust, a tiny lift of his right shoulder before a cut. His feet too carried a message, a tensing of the left which dug his sandal into the sand and which meant he was about to lunge.

Small things, but on them could depend my life.

Metal clashed as we engaged, shields taking the fury of the blows, swords flashing, lifting to fall, to lift again in a bursting storm of energy. A slash scarred the armour on my right arm, my own blade, sweeping upwards, catching the unprotected flesh on his inner bicep. He backed, blood dripping from the wound to stain his right side.

'Habet!' screamed the crowd. 'Habet!'

The wound was nothing, a shallow gash which had not reached the tendons, but it made him wary. Cautiously he circled me, waiting for the attack, the slight advantage it would give. Edging to my right I ran forward, swaying to the left as we neared, my shield a barrier which caught his sword and pushed it aside as my own blade thrust at his body. A thrust which blunted the point against his shield as he jerked it to the right. Instantly I lunged again, this time upwards towards the face beneath the helmet, my defence careless as I exposed the left side of my body. Metal rang as my sword hit his lifted shield and his own blade dropped then lanced upwards towards the target I displayed. A blow which missed as I twisted, my left arm clamping down on his right, my sword falling to stab upwards, the edge grating on the lower edge of the shield which he dropped, too late to prevent the steel plunging into his stomach.

A twist and it was done.

Beneath the helmet his sweating face went suddenly blank. He looked at me, then at his ripped abdomen, the intestines like greasy ropes as they hung from the gash. Then, his eyes rolling upwards, he fell, dead before he hit the sand.

And I was the darling of Rome.

CHAPTER TEN

On the bed the woman stirred and said, "Atilus, how can I make you wholly mine?'

Once there would have been an answer, but I was no longer a slave to be bought and sold like a sack of grain. Now, as the most popular gladiator in Rome, I could afford to pick and choose with whom I spent my time. And I had chosen well. Dollitia Flavius was rich and had high connections; through her I could gain access to the Emperor. As I had not been sent for by Nero, it was the only way.

Now, like a satiated animal, she sprawled on the bed watching as I dressed.

'Atilus?'

'Domina, there is nothing I would like more than to spend the rest of my life at your side.'

'You're a liar,' she said calmly. 'But a good one. Almost I believe you mean what you say. Unfortunately there are complications.'

Her husband, for one, a senator who spent much of his time on his estates in Etruria. Her relatives who, while turning a blind eye to her peccadillos, would resent the introduction of a gladiator into the family circle. And she had two children who were old enough to be conscious of their dignity.

Not that it mattered. I wanted only one thing from the woman and she knew it. And, knowing it, she had made me pay for the service in coin of her own choosing. Not that it had been a hardship. Even though no longer a girl her body held a rich promise which made it easy for me to satisfy her wants. And yet, looking at her, I wished that it had been Racilia who lay watching me.

Thought of her made me impatient, but I let nothing of it show in my voice or expression.

'Domina, shouldn't you be getting ready?'

'The party?' Her sniff held contempt. 'Thrasea Valens is a bore.'

'But you said—'

'The Emperor would attend,' she interrupted. 'Yes, I know. And that's all you want from me, isn't it, Atilus? To be introduced to Nero. Is that why you sought my bed?'

She had sensed the truth and, for a moment, her face displayed anger. Then she laughed and shrugged.

'Well, I can't blame you for that, and at least you've been honest. And if I refuse you, others will oblige. Go and bathe now, be patient until I am ready.'

* * * * * * *

Thrasea Valens was a broad, corpulant man, almost bald, his eyes a pale hazel, deep-set under bushy brows. As slaves ushered us into the atrium, he came forward to greet us, hands extended, the fingers bright with gems.

Smiling he said, 'Dollitia Flavius, my house is honoured.'

'It was good of you to accommodate me, Thrasea. We have drifted apart of late. A fault for which I must take the blame.'

'These things happen, my dear. Marriage, children, the cares of running a household.' His shrug was expressive, and I sensed that once they had been more than friends. 'And your companion?'

'Atilus Cindras.'

'Atilus? The gladiator?'

His surprise was genuine; I did not look the part. My hair was longer than normal for a man of my profession and it had been dressed in the Grecian style. I wore silk and gold, and fine sandals were on my feet. In any company I would have been taken for the scion of some rich family—the scar on my cheek the result of some military wound.

'The same,' said Dollitia. 'He is an old friend of the Emperor. Has he arrived?'

Nero was in an inner chamber listening to music played by a group of young girls. He sat on a bench, beating time with his hands, his eyes misted with inner thoughts. Warned by Thrasea's uplifted hand, we waited until the end of the piece then moved quietly forward.

'Beautiful!' Nero clapped his hands, his face beaming with pleasure. 'A delicate air delicately played. You agree?'

'Music worthy of the gods,' said a man standing to one side. He was young, his face marred by acne, his lips moist and slack. 'But what else could it be when composed by a master?'

'The Muses themselves must have guided your creation,' said another, eager to add his flattery. 'Never before have I heard such sweet cadences of pure harmony.'

Nero ignored them, looking to where an older man sat on a stool. 'Gaius?'

Shrugging the man said, 'It holds undoubted merit, Caesar, but it was a little weak in the third passage.'

'It is?'

'As you yourself mentioned when first you showed me the composition. As I remember, you decided to leave it for later correction. Even so, it would take a shrewd ear to detect the fault, as our friends have shown.'

'And for their failure to spot the weakness they should be punished,' said Nero. 'Unless an artist has true critical praise how is he to know the extent of his achievement? What penalty would be suitable, Gaius?'

'To deny them your company for a week. That, Caesar, would be to rob them of your perfection.'

Gaius Petronius was a man in his middle age with a smoothly cynical face and eyes which held a strange weariness. A man of proven merit he had turned his energies to the pursuit of pleasure, and now held the unofficial position of Nero's arbiter of elegance. A clever man who knew better than to drown the Emperor with endless flattery, and whose opinion was the more valued because of his pointed criticism.

A man I felt it would be wise to know and whose friendship it would be advantageous to gain. At dinner I had the chance to study him more closely and to appreciate his skill.

I ate little and drank less. The wine was rich and potent, swilled by some but not, I noticed, by Petronius, who was as abstemious as myself.

Someone mentioned the recent games and Nero slammed his hand down hard on the table.

'Blood!' he said. 'Blood and barbaric butchery is all that appeals to the mob. I've tried to teach them gentler arts but they would have none of it. They demand their beasts and gladiators, and have no time for music and dancing. At times I wonder if they are worth my concern.'

'You strive too hard to please, Caesar,' said one of the syco-phants. 'It would teach the public a lesson if you were to refuse them the fruits of your genius.'

'In Greece you would be truly honoured.' A thin man with a weak mouth and a toga now stained with wine set down his goblet with an unsteady hand. 'The home of culture and gracious living. There the air is sweetened with music and intel-ligent discourse, and men watch plays instead of men killing each other. Only in Greece can artistic genius be really appreci-ated.'

Nero nodded, not answering, his eyes following the lithe figure of a slave. A young girl, her hair a shimmering mass of ebon strands, her simple gown doing little to hide the ripe femi-ninity it covered.

'A lovely creature,' he mused. 'She would make an amusing episode, Gaius, as I'm sure you will agree.'

'As you will agree, Caesar, that an unripe fruit holds little juice,' said Petronius casually. 'In any case her hips are far too broad to attract any man of discernment. Only a slave would wish to ride such a mare.'

'Of course.' Nero waved a negligent hand. 'I was testing you, Gaius, but your eye is as sharp as my own and, as always, you are right. Thrasea, have you no Greek wine?'

It was heavy stuff, thick with resin, perfumed and sickly with honey. Added to the rest, it went quickly to a young man's head.

Narva Plancius had been spoiled from birth and, high in Nero's favour, felt free to say anything he wished. Now, looking at me, he sneered.

'Thrasea, I wonder at your discretion. To have invited a common gladiator to sit with the Emperor shows how little you understand artistic delicacy.'

I waited for Nero to comment, but he remained silent, one gemmed hand toying with his goblet. His eyes, I thought, held a faint amusement.

'In Greece he would not be tolerated,' said the thin man. 'We have no time for barbarians who are little more than butchers. We have theatres, not arenas, and despite demands from the local garrisons, we have continued to reject the games.'

'How long do you imagine you will be able to resist the demands, Polyclitus?' Petronius's tone was ironic as he carefully selected a nut and crushed it with bronze tongs. 'Greece is a province of Rome. As yet we have treated you with courtesy and respected your wishes, but the amphitheatres will come and you will have to learn to like them.'

'Like them?' More than a little drunk, the man was careless. 'How can any civilised race enjoy such spectacles?'

He was on dangerous ground, but his wits were too fuddled for him to realise it. Nero, for all his affectations and pretences, was a Roman, as were others in the assembly. One of them, a man who had previously remained silent, glared his anger as he reared from the couch.

'Are you saying that Rome isn't civilised?'

'The proof—'

'What proof? The fact that you mincing Greeks spout verse and tremble at the sight of a little blood? To me that is proof of your weakness. If you hadn't forgotten your manhood, you wouldn't have fallen to the legions. Greeks!' He glowered and snatched up his wine. 'Disgusting boy-lovers! Degenerate filth! A man's seed belongs in the belly of a woman, not in the rectum of a man!'

'You're old-fashioned, Quintilius,' said Petronius mildly. 'Things change.'

'Maybe, but the old times were good enough for me. Then a man worked hard and no one minded a little manure on his boots. Now it's all fine silks and perfume. Are you telling me that the men who built Rome were wrong?'

'Drink your wine, Quintilius, and calm down,' said Petronius. 'I'm merely saying that a man should have the right to seek pleasure in his own way. What else does life have to offer? And customs change with time. Take the games, for example. Once they were slaves fighting in honour of the dead. Now we have wild beast shows and all the rest of it. The mob demands novelty, but I fail to see how watching a girl being raped by an animal can make a man a good soldier. Can you?'

'It gets him used to the sight of blood and pain,' said Quintilius. 'It hardens his resolve so that, in time of war, he will not flinch from combat.'

'That is the theory,' admitted Petronius. 'But how many watching would make any kind of a soldier at all? Certainly not the women, and they are as eager as any to witness the games.'

'Women breed men and, if they are hard, so will be their sons.' Quintilius slammed down his empty goblet. 'To me it is obvious, but I can't bandy words with you, Gaius Petronius. The achievements of Rome speak for themselves.'

The talk dissolved into generalities and I began to get a little anxious. As yet Nero had not spoken to me or acknowledged our old relationship. Dollitia had given me the opportunity to meet him, but the rest was up to me and I looked for a way to attract his attention.

Narva Plancius provided it. Eager to make himself the centre of attention, he fell into my hands.

'There is an odd taint in the air,' he announced to no one

in particular. 'I've smelt it before in a slaughterhouse. Surely, Thrasea, you don't kill beasts on your premises?'

'Of course not, Narva.'

'Then why the smell? Can't you notice it? To me it is very obvious.' The fool sniffed at the air. 'It seems to be close.'

He was getting at me and I knew it. Silently thanking the gods for what they had provided, I rose and stepped to where he lounged. Gripping his arm, I lifted him from the couch and slammed him down on his feet. Thrusting my hand beneath his nose, I snapped, 'Smell it. Go on, take a good sniff. Can you smell blood?'

My other hand was on his shoulder and I could feel bone beneath my fingers. He winced as I increased the pressure.

'No,' he muttered. 'No, I can't.'

'Then it must be something else you smell. Agreed?'

'I—'

'Yourself, perhaps?'

Sweat broke out on his face and, squirming, he appealed to the Emperor. 'Please, noble Caesar, help me.'

'Against Atilus?' Nero shrugged, his voice bearing a casual amusement. 'I think not, Narva. He is an old friend.'

The acknowledgement I had hoped for and, hearing it, the young man blanched.

'I—' he stammered. 'I didn't know. Nero, forgive me!'

'But of course I forgive you, Narva Plancius. However, I think it would be best for you to leave Rome. The legions in Judea can always use good officers, and I'm sure that your father can spare you for, say, five years.' Nero smiled, amused at his jest, his suggestion which was an order. 'Now you may leave us. Petronius, remind me to have Burras arrange the young man's posting.'

Slaves cleared away the debris of the meal and passed bowls of water in which we washed our hands. The thin man, shaken by what had happened, sat sombre and silent. Dollitia, in an effort to get the conversation going, mentioned an item of news she had received from her husband.

'Caius discovered something unusual when he paid a visit to Perusia. He attended the games there and said they had actually had a woman fight against a man. A woman, can you imagine it? Atilus, is it possible?'

It was more than possible, it was common practice, and I said so. Girls dressed as Diana and armed with bows would be set against African pygmies dressed in skins and carrying spears. At some of the events women depicting Amazons would fight against men and boys. And often a Master of Games would re-enact the Rape of the Sabines when a group of women would be attacked by a crowd of men—the final conclusion of which greatly amused the crowd.

Impatiently Dollitia shook her head.

'No, I don't mean that. This woman actually fought as a gladiator.'

'Are you sure?'

'It happened. They didn't know she was a woman, of course, but she lost and was killed, and when they dragged her from the arena they found out. The town was full of it, Caius said. They talked of nothing else in the baths and you can imagine the comments. At times men can be rather disgusting, but what I want to know is how such a thing is possible. I mean—a woman!'

She was thinking of herself, of her own, unmistakably feminine body, but I had seen other women who were nothing like she was. Hard, tough slaves who toiled in the fields from dawn to dusk, their breasts withered, their hands as broad and tough as those of a man. If they cropped their hair and deepened their voices, some of them might just might get by as a man.

But in the arena?

'She would have had to be free,' I said. 'A volunteer. And she would have had a trusted servant who could keep her secret. A male. Did she have one?'

'I don't know. Caius didn't say.'

'How would such a woman fight?' said Petronius thoughtfully. 'Certainly not as a *retiarius*.'

'Not unless she lacked breasts.' Nero was excited, his eyes holding a bright sparkle, thinking, perhaps, of soft mounds bobbing, bouncing, quivering masses in constant motion. 'What then? Atilus, tell us.'

'You're thinking of a normal woman,' I pointed out. 'But she could have been a hermaphrodite and neither fully a man or a woman. In that case, she could have had only very small breasts and narrow hips. Or she could have been stocky and almost shapeless. If she had been strong, she could have worn a cuirass and fought as a *cruppellarius*. In any case she must have been a freak.'

'Because she wanted to fight in the arena?' Dollitia was sharp.

'That too, but I was thinking of her physique.' Some nuts rested in a silver bowl which had been left on the table and I picked up a couple, crushing them in my hands before picking at the kernels. 'But you have a point—why should any normal woman want to fight as a gladiator in the amphitheatre?'

'Perhaps because she was tired of fighting in bed,' said Dollitia. 'That's an arena too, you know. Or perhaps she had a hatred of men which drove her to kill.'

'In that case, there are easier ways,' said Petronius dryly. 'And far safer. But we speculate to no purpose; the woman is dead and we shall never know what drove her to do as she did. I agree with Atilus, she must have been a freak. Certainly she was a rarity.'

'A pity.' Nero toyed with a goblet of wine, moving it in small circles so that the liquid it contained swirled high to almost slop over the rim. 'I would like to see women fight each other.'

'As gladiators?' Quintilius snorted his contempt. 'That's ridiculous. They would be laughed from the amphitheatre.'

'Would they?' murmured Nero. For a moment he stared at his wine as if, within it, he saw visions. Then looking at Quintilius he said, 'Why? What makes you say that? How can you be sure?'

'Because it stands to reason. A woman's place is in the home. Female gladiators would ridicule the games. They would make a mockery of the whole thing. No, it isn't possible. The public would never stand for it.'

'The public!' Nero's face tightened in anger, his eyes tinged with red. 'Always must I consider the public. They sneer at my singing, deride my plays, even accuse me of murdering my mother. Yes, even that, and still I must consider them. I tell you that at times I weary of the people. With my talents I could earn a living anywhere in the Empire. Why then should I remain a slave to the people?'

'Because they need you,' said Dollitia Flavius quickly. 'Because we all need you.'

'You are kind to say so, my dear.' Nero touched a scrap of scented fabric to his eyes. 'But is it true?'

He was acting, using us for an audience, waiting for the storm of assurance which followed his question. Fullsome praise which likened him to the sun, the absence of which would darken the world. The thin man went so far as to drop to his knees and offer his life to the gods if Nero would condescend to remain Emperor. A dangerous bit of flattery as I, who knew Nero's cruel whims, was aware.

'Your life, Polyclitus?' Nero sighed and again dabbed at his eyes. 'You shame my weakness with your resolve. Very well, the gods accept your sacrifice. Atilus, have you a dagger?'

A test? No one was permitted to be armed in the presence of Nero afraid as he was of assassination. He seemed to relax a little as I shook my head.

'No? Well, it doesn't matter. Use your hands.'

Polyclitus cringed as I rested my fingers around his throat, my thumbs firm on his spine. Nero watched, his face avid, then Petronius touched his arm and said something in a low voice.

'Again, my arbiter, you are right,' said Nero. 'It would be in bad taste to kill the man in so crude a manner. Polyclitus, you are fortunate, the gods do not want your life, but only an offering to Jupiter. Tomorrow be at the temple with a thousand pieces of gold.'

Brokenly the man thanked him for his kindness, then went to

console himself with wine. Thrasea, eager to break the tension, summoned musicians, their low notes providing an accompaniment to the resumed conversation. Nero gestured for me to sit at his side.

'It has been many years, old friend, since I saw you last. Now tell me, what can I do for you?'

'Domine, your favour is enough.'

'You haven't changed, Atilus. You know, when I saw you in the arena, I thought I looked at a ghost. My late mother—' He broke off, sighing. 'A strong woman but a dominating one. I shall miss her. I would like to do something to perpetuate her memory. What should it be? A new temple? A monument? A city founded in her name?'

Petronius said, 'An excessive display of grief would not be in the Roman manner. Alsom the things you mention would cost a great deal of money. In my opinion the public would prefer a play in the Grecian style which would carry a moral.'

And would also be cheap. Nero smiled as he considered it, then reluctantly shook his head.

'No. On second thought I think I will allow my dear, departed mother to sink into oblivion. The public are not ready for such delicate entertainment. They demand stronger meat and expect me to provide it for them. But what more can I do?' For a moment he sat, musing, then abruptly snapped his fingers. 'I have it! That woman, the one who fought as a gladiator, have you heard of anything like that before, Atilus?'

'No, Caesar.'

'Gaius?'

Petronius shook his head. 'Such a thing would be in deplorable taste.'

'True, but what do the public know of such delicacy? Women gladiators would be a novelty to introduce to Rome and, always, the mob demands novelty.' Lifting a hand Nero gnawed at a finger. His eyes held a wild expression as of a man being tempted and about to yield to the temptation whimsical though it might be. 'Quintilius is old and out of touch with public taste,' he mused. 'He said that women gladiators would be laughed from the arena, but I think he is wrong. I shall prove him to be wrong. To Rome I will give a new experience. Atilus, I want you to arrange it.'

'Female gladiators?'

'Yes.' Like a child with a new toy Nero was entranced at the prospect. Enamoured too, perhaps, by the shock it would give to the old, staid families. 'Who better to do it? The gods must have sent you here tonight. Atilus, you will start at once!'

CHAPTER ELEVEN

Looking at his wine, Agonestes said, 'So you are now an imperial agent, Atilus. Congratulations.'

'You don't approve?'

'Frankly, no. Was Nero drunk when he made the offer? Surely he couldn't have been serious.'

A suspicion I had entertained, but which dissolved when money and credentials had been supplied. For reasons of his own Nero wanted women to fight and fall, to bleed and die to the shrieking plaudits of a mob. Either he wanted to gain popularity or, in some distorted manner, to take revenge on his dead mother. I couldn't decide which and it made no difference. Nero would go his own way, and if I hadn't taken the job, someone else would.

'You can't be blamed for taking any profit that's going,' said Agonestes when I had pointed that out. 'But what's his real motive? Nero isn't all that fond of women despite his affairs with Poppaea and Acte, not to mention a host of others. I think he could be a little jealous of them. I know for a fact that he often dresses up as a girl and goes to bed with an ex-gladiator. Pythagoras, you know him?'

'No.'

'He made his mark while you were away and now he's closer to Nero than honey to bread. Of course,' mused Agonestes, 'Nero could be trying to debase the games so badly the public will turn from them to his own ideas of entertainment. Not that it matters. How are you going to set about it?'

'That's why I asked you to join me. Any ideas?'

We sat in a room I had hired in an inn, a clean place run by a widow with the help of her two sons, grown boys with an inclination to join the legions. It lay at the foot of the Capitoline Hill, and did a brisk trade with those having business at the temple of Jupiter on the summit.

'Women,' mused Agonestes. 'You want them tough, hard, and vicious. How about the brothels at Misenum? Those whores have to be hard to take what the sailors give them.'

'It's a different kind of fighting,' I said dryly.

'True, and those old bags are on their last legs anyway.' Agonestes sipped and sat, thinking. His chair was by the window, and afternoon sunlight gilded his hair and threw his profile into sharp relief. From the street below came a continuous susurration of noise, the pad of feet, conversation, cries from the vendors of charms and incense together with those of the sellers of wine and cooked snacks. 'You could try the slave market.'

'And training?'

'That doesn't matter so much,' he pointed out. 'All Nero wants is a show. The women will be set one against the other, so skill isn't too important. Just as long as they have the will to fight, the rest will follow. The main thing is to have some pairs ready as soon as possible.'

'Good, I'm glad you see it that way.'

'You've already thought it out,' he accused. 'Atilus, what's in your mind?'

'I need help,' I told him bluntly. 'That's why I really sent for you. I want you to take charge here in Rome while I search for appropriate contenders. There's a small house with a garden which would do as a training ground. Hire a few slaves and some men to act as guards and we're away.'

'We?'

'I can't do it wholly alone, Agonestes. How are you placed? Found a new, rich patron yet?'

'There's someone.'

'Who could drop you at any time. Work in with me and stay out of the arena. I'll arrange about money and the house.' Reaching out I took his hand. 'Agonestes, I'm asking you as a friend.'

'I would rather you asked me as a lover.' His fingers closed tightly on my own. 'Why not, Atilus? You know I've always liked you.'

'And if we were to meet face to face on the sand?' I eased free my hand as he made no answer. 'You'll do it?'

For a moment he hesitated, then nodded. 'And you?'

'I'm off to Perusia. That woman could have been a freak, but there's a chance there could be others with similar inclinations. I've a letter to one of the local *duumvirs*, Aquinas Rebilus. He might be able to help. In the meantime find what you can.'

It was growing late when Heraculis and I rode from the city and headed down the Flamminian Way. Nero had provided me with a courier's badge which entitled me to change mounts at the posting stations, and so we made good time, reaching Ocriculum before midnight. At Mevania we swung north, stayed the night at Urvinium, and finally reached Perusia at noon a few days after leaving Rome.

Leaving Heraculis at an inn, I went to the house of Aquinas Rebilus and presented myself together with my letter. He was about to eat his mid-day meal and, after one glance at the official seal, invited me to join him.

The repast was simple; bread, honey, cold meat, and a dish of fruit, accompanied by a rough wine. His wife, a patrician of late middle age and his daughter, a sombre girl with dark and haunted eyes a little younger than myself, ate with us, afterwards withdrawing to leave us alone.

Only then did he read the letter. He was a stocky man with a bluff, no-nonsense manner, a farmer who had married money, and who had gained local prominence. He looked at me from beneath bushy eyebrows.

'So you're Atilus Cindras, friend of the Emperor and engaged on official business, eh?'

'That's right.'

'And I'm instructed to give you all possible aid.' He puffed out his cheeks a little.

Patiently I said, 'Yes.'

'But in reference to what? The letter doesn't say.' His eyes bulged as I told him. 'Women to fight as gladiators? I don't believe it. The thing's incredible!'

'No,' I said. 'Not incredible. In fact it's already happened here in Perusia. Surely you know about it?'

'An isolated incident.'

'Perhaps.'

'The woman looked more like a man than many men I've seen. Cropped hair, a weathered face, arms as thick as thighs. It was impossible to tell she was a female. Even her voice was as deep as my own. She—'

'Fought as a *cruppellarius*,' I interrupted. 'She was a volunteer and had a male servant to attend her. Am I right?' His nod confirmed my deductions. 'Is the servant still in the vicinity?'

'I'm not sure. He could be.' Rebilus made a gesture of distaste. 'The thing was a scandal. A disgrace. There is no law against it, of course, but no woman should fight in the arena. The whole thing is best forgotten.'

'That isn't possible.' I touched the letter lying before him. 'The Emperor is interested and has sent me to investigate. If there are others like her, I must find them. Your help would be appreciated.'

Help which couldn't be refused unless Aquinas Rebilus wanted to run into trouble, but I didn't remind him of the fact. Willing co-operation was worth more than reluctant obedience.

Slowly he said, 'What do you want me to do?'

'Announce that I am here from Rome looking for women who are willing to fight as gladiators. The willingness is enough, they don't have to be skilled, but I will select those suitable.'

'And you really hope to get applicants?' He shook his head, a man baffled by the strange turn things were taking. 'No woman in her right mind would volunteer herself for such a thing.'

Privately I agreed with him, but everything had to be tried.

'Just do it, sir. Have them report to me at the amphitheatre. In the meantime I would like to see your Master of Games.'

Varus Horatius was a dour veteran with a scarred face and drooping eyelids which gave him the appearance of a vulture. He had joined the legions as soon as he was old enough, rising from the ranks to become first a decanus in charge of ten men, then a centurion. Serving his thirty years, he had been discharged and had chosen to remain in Italy. He had been given his present post three years earlier.

'Atilus!' His grip was firm as we saluted each other. 'I've heard of you. Didn't you fight at Interamna?'

'Among other places, yes.'

'And won the *rudis* from Nero himself?'

'That was years ago.'

'You beat a famed *retiarius* and then took on a couple of Thracians—come and have a drink!'

'With pleasure,' I said. 'But could I have a look at the amphitheatre first?'

The building was small, as I had expected, built of wood above stone, the stands consisting of three tiers rising steeply above the podium. The actual arena was more round than oval, and about a hundred and twenty feet wide.

'It isn't much compared to what you have in Rome,' said Horatius as he showed me around. 'But we usually manage to put on a good show. At the last one we had a score of bulls, five lions, seven bears, and three dozen wild dogs. Five *bestiarii* got killed and a total of thirty-eight pairs fought in three days.'

Not bad for a provincial town with limited facilities and money. Horatius had put on a gladiatorial display many larger communities would envy. I said so and he beamed his pleasure at my praise.

'A man tries to do his best.'

'You're wasted here. Tell me, do you have trouble finding contenders?'

'Not much. The travelling *lanistae* make a point of coming

with their troupes of fighters, and there's always a few volunteers. Some of them are pretty poor stuff, I'd admit, but they help to bulk out the programme. You ready for that drink now?'

Over wine I mentioned the woman.

'That was Baetrix,' he said. 'I never knew her real name and I didn't guess that she was a woman. She'd fought a couple of times before, nothing special, but plenty of slogging, and good enough for the mornings when things were a little slow. I matched her against a *laquearius* and he got her with his lasso. Down she went, but instead of waiting for the verdict she reared and made a grab at his balls. Got them too from the way he yelled, but couldn't carry it through. Before she could give a real twist he'd got her with the trident. Rammed it straight into her eyes.'

'And?'

'That's about all there is to it. After she was dragged out and stripped they found she was missing something. Mind you, it was all that she was missing; the bitch was as strong as a horse.'

'She was a woman?' I insisted. 'No chance of her having been a catamite?'

'No. I thought of that and examined the body myself. I served in the east for a time and know what a sheared man looks like. A eunuch gets fat if he's had his privates sliced off when young. If he has the lot removed later on, he stays much the same, aside from the fact he has to squat when making water or splash his legs. No, it was a woman right enough, Atilus, you can take my word for it. I've known too many in my time to be mistaken.'

I ordered more wine, Falernian, and insisted on paying for it. As he drank I told Horatius the purpose of my visit.

He choked and I had to beat him on the back before he could talk.

'Women gladiators? It's unnatural. Men are born to fight, it's their job, but women are something else. It won't work. It can't. Even if you find them, it'll have a bad effect on the others. You know how things are before a fight. Knowing women are around, stripping off, getting ready—' he broke off shaking his head. 'I don't like it.'

'It's not what you like,' I said. 'And it's not what I like, but it's what Nero wants, and I'm stuck with the job. Now, can you help me to find women who are willing to fight? The *duumvir* is going to make an announcement, but you might have personal knowledge of possible applicants.'

Horatius helped himself to more wine.

'If it was men you wanted, there'd be no problem. There are always some young fools wanting to try their skill and not knowing what it's all about. But women are different. Let me think, now—they'll be paired against other women?'

'Yes.'

'And it'll just be a show?'

'Yes,' I lied. Once in the arena, they would kill or be killed, but first I had to get them into the arena. 'You know anyone?'

'I don't know, but I'll pass the word. There could be a few recalcitrant slaves their owners would sell cheap. They might fight if you offered them their freedom. Then others might do it just for the chance to get to Rome. Leave it with me, Atilus. Where are you staying?' He nodded as I told him. 'A decent place. You won't lack for anything you might fancy.' His wink spoke volumes. 'Now let's have some more wine.'

It was dusk when I rejoined Heraculis to find that Aquinas Rebilus had invited me to dinner. An invitation I could hardly refuse. The reason became obvious when, after a meal of boiled mutton, assorted vegetables, and a compote of fruit his wife began to question me about Rome.

'Is it true that the Emperor sleeps on silk sheets,' she gushed.

'And that he has fifteen young slave-boys from Greece to sing him lullabyes?'

'A score, madam, not fifteen,' I told her seriously. 'And, yes, he does sleep on silk.'

'Silk from the far east or that from the Aegean isle of Kos?'

'From the far east, madam.'

'You're wearing silk, Atilus,' said the daughter. Her tone was envious. 'I'd love to wear silk. Are you married?'

'No.'

'Betrothed, then?'

'Natalia, mind your manners!' Her mother was quick to scold. Perhaps a little too quick and I saw the hurt in the haunted eyes. To me she said, 'You must forgive the child. We have few visitors from Rome and she forgets herself in her eagerness to hear the news. Aquinas! Our guest has an empty goblet!'

Dutifully he poured. The room was empty of slaves who would normally have served me, for reasons I could guess.

'And Lollia Poppaea? You have seen her? Do tell us what she is like.'

The woman wanted gossip, not news, scandal, not dry items of information, and I gave her what she wanted, inventing when my knowledge was exhausted, but never stepping over the bounds of discretion. Half the people I mentioned did not exist. The stories I told about them held no more substance than the yarns told by wandering entertainers who spun their romances by firelight or smoking lamps in low taverns.

But when it came to Nero and other prominent persons, I did not hesitate to flatter.

The Emperor was superb in every way, the nearest thing to a living god our world has ever known. The beauty of Lollia Poppaea surpassed even that of Helen of ancient Troy. Petronius was a master of gracious living and the arts. Even Seneca got his share of praise, though I thought little of the man. The reports the *duumvir* might send to Rome would hold nothing which could make me enemies.

Inevitably we spoke of the arena.

'What is it like, Atilus?' Natalia leaned forward and it was not by accident that her hands held the stola taut so as to reveal the swell of her breasts. A child her mother might consider her, but to me she was a full-grown woman, and one who should long since have been married. 'Do many women seek out the gladiators after the fights?'

'You have your own amphitheatre,' I reminded. 'You must know what goes on.'

'Natalia is not allowed to see the games,' said her mother primly. 'I've seen too many girls sullied by groping hands to permit it. It is a disgrace that the virtue of women is not respected at such times. When Natalia marries, she will be pure.'

'If I marry,' said the girl bitterly. 'And that will be never unless you provide me with a good dowry. And the longer you make me wait, the larger it will have to be.' With a sudden change of mood she said, quickly, 'Atilus, if you married, would you take your wife to Rome?'

'If I marry, yes.'

'If?' She frowned. 'A man shouldn't wait too long before he marries, should he, father. If he does there could be talk that he is—well, you know.'

'I know that it's time you went to bed,' said her mother firmly. 'Be off now, Natalia.'

'Must I?'

'Do as I say!' As the girl reluctantly obeyed, her mother said, "The girl is a problem, Atilus. Our only child and we have spoiled her.'

'You should let a husband do that.'

'There is plenty of time for that.' With a gesture the woman dismissed her daughter's problems. 'Now tell me of the latest fashions. The Grecian influence is very strong, I hear.'

It was late when we finally rose and Aquinas insisted that I stay the night as his guest. The room to which a slave guided me was small, bleak, more of a cell than a sleeping chamber, and I regretted the lost comfort of the inn and the pleasures Horatius had hinted were available.

Natalia was willing to replace them.

She stole into my room like a ghost, resting her fingers on my lips as, roused by a creak from the door, I reared upright on the bed.

'It's all right, Atilus,' she whispered. 'It's only me.'

'What do you want?'

A stupid question; there was only one reason why she had come to me like a thief in the night, and she gave proof of it as, with a quick movement, she slipped out of her nightgown and slid into the bed. Her skin was cold and she trembled a little as she lay beside me.

'Atilus?'

'No.'

'Why not?' Her voice held a strained note of hurt. 'Am I so ugly that you don't want to touch me?'

The wanting was there, I could feel it as my body responded to her nearness. Cold though her skin was, it held softness, and the mounds of her breasts matched the swell of her hips, the tempting curve of her thighs. Yet a memory came between us, that of her haunted eyes and the desperation they had held.

'Natalia, you should be married. You must insist that a suitor is found for you.' The moon threw light into the chamber and, in its glow, I gently caressed her hair. 'Is there no one you would like to share your life?'

'Yes, Atilus, you.' She pressed against me, her body warming with a demanding heat. 'Please, darling. Please!' Then, as I touched her, she drew in her breath in sudden pain.

A virgin! I should have known.

Sensing my withdrawal she lifted herself on one elbow and stared at me. The moonlight illuminated her face, deepening her eyes, turning the tears which came from them into a stream of pearls.

'Am I so repulsive, Atilus, that even a—'

'Common gladiator doesn't want you?' I was curt as I completed her sentence. 'We are men, Natalia, not beasts. And you are far from ugly, as you well know.'

'Then—'

'You don't want me, girl. You want escape. You're hoping for what? That I shall fall in love with you and take you with me to Rome? That, once I have had you, I shall feel honour bound to marry you? Forget it, Natalia, life isn't like that.'

I was hurtful, but deliberately so. Had she been other than she was, already we would have been lovers. But she was a thing of fragile glass, and to take and use her would leave only hurt.

Quietly I said, 'Girl, you need more strength. Your mother dominates you. Defy her. Find a man you like and let him know how you feel. Tempt him, but do not yield until you are his wife. But choose carefully. Make certain he is someone of whom your father will approve.'

'He will do as mother tells him.'

'A Roman is master in his own house. Remind him of that.' Gently I touched her cheeks, wiping away the tears. 'And don't underestimate yourself. With what you have to offer a man, you could be a mother within a year.'

'Atilus!'

'Go!' I was abruptly harsh. 'Leave me, girl. Don't be stupid!'

For a moment she stared at me and then, softly, she left my side. The door creaked after her as she padded away and for a long time I lay staring at the moonlight on the wall wondering if I'd been a fool.

CHAPTER TWELVE

A week later a dozen women lined up in the amphitheatre for my inspection. For me it had been a hard seven days, with the *duumvir* becoming more patronising, his wife full of talk about dowries, and Natalia making herself conspicuously absent. After the first night I'd slept at the inn, giving business as the reason for refusing further hospitality, but I could not afford to ignore all the invitations to dinner.

I groaned as I read another delivered to the inn by a slave; Heraculis brought it to the baths where I sweated out recent fatigue.

Varus Horatius had told me of the possibility of finding a suitable woman on an outlying farm and I had ridden over to examine the prospect. The journey had been a waste of time. The girl was a cripple, one foot twisted, her body like a reed. Her owner, a scowling man who was kinder to his pigs than to his slaves, asked a ridiculous price and was offended at my answer.

'You primping degenerates from Rome don't know good material when you see it,' he stormed. 'That girl can work all day with only a bowl of porridge at noon. She's strong too, I've had her hitched to a plough and she can carry as much as a man. Just beat her a little now and again and she'll do anything you want.'

'Keep working her like that and she won't last a month.'

'Why, you sleek swine! Are you telling me how to handle my own property?'

'You're not fit to own a dog,' I told him. 'I'm reporting this to the *duumvir*. There are laws regarding the treatment of slaves and I'll see they are enforced.'

He turned purple and snatched up a flail. I almost dodged the first blow, catching it on the back of a shoulder, and as he charged again I stepped aside to knock him rolling in a patch of stinking mud. As he rose, nursing his jaw, covered with liquid manure, I said, harshly, 'You've just attacked an imperial agent of Rome. Take better care of your slaves or I'll accuse you of rebellion. I'll be back in a week to see how they're getting on.'

A lie, but he wouldn't know that, and if nothing else it would restrain him for a time.

His fall had spattered me with slime, which together with the blow and the ache caused by unaccustomed riding made me ready for the baths. Perusia had a decent installation for public use, but I used the private one recommended by Horatius. Female slaves did the massage and, for a fee, would do far more. One of them was trying to arouse me, letting her hands linger as they slid over my stomach and thighs, leaning well over so that I could see the generous breasts beneath her loose gown. She straightened, frowning, when Heraculis arrived with the invitation.

Dismissing her with a casual slap on the rear, he said, 'You're moving in high society, master. The girl isn't bad to look at and you could do worse. Aquinas Rebilus owns a great deal of property and the dowry would be large.'

'One day I'm going to clip your tongue.'

'Then how would I be able to give you advice, master?' He grinned, unabashed. 'Shall I send word to the *duumvir* that you will accept his invitation?'

'No. Make an excuse. Tell him that I'm called away on business.'

'Better to say that you are examining potential females at the inn,' he suggested. 'The Emperor's commands must be obeyed no matter at what personal inconvenience, and you'll regret the lost opportunity of again meeting his lovely wife and daughter.

You could send a small gift as a token of your esteem.'

'Such as?'

'A bolt of cloth or some perfume. Or an adornment of some kind. I have met a trader who deals in such things.'

'And who will give you a generous commission, no doubt.'

'If he doesn't, master,' said Heraculis blandly, 'he won't make the sale. And to make the tale a good one, you should really be at work. That woman who was massaging you, for example? She is worth investigating.'

'Forget her. Any news from Horatius?'

'He'll have the women ready for you to look at tomorrow.' Heraculis filled his palm with warm, scented oil and, as he resumed the interrupted massage, said, 'Master, I've been thinking. Men wouldn't want to see women in the arena who look like ordinary gladiators. There wouldn't be any novelty in it. If women are to be used at all, why not make it obvious what they are?'

'You've a low mind, Heraculis.'

'So have most men, master. You've heard them cheer when the *trinqui* are being pulled down by the beasts. They always yell loudest when it's a girl being torn apart.' His fingers probed the bruised flesh of my shoulder. 'A pity you can't buy a few of the women who work here. They would make a wonderful show.'

He was giving voice to something I had already considered, but first the initial barrier had to be surmounted. Nothing could be decided until I had material on which to work.

In the morning light of the following day I looked at what had been found. As gladiatorial material they were far from promising.

'They're all that is available, Atilus,' said Varus Horatius. He was apologetic. 'I've combed the entire area. Two only came in answer to the announcements, the rest are slaves. Their owners are waiting over there.' He gestured to where some men stood huddled at one side of the arena.

Ignoring them I studied the women. All were poorly dressed

in gowns of rough sacking, their feet bare, their hair long and lank with dirt and grease. The two volunteers could not be distinguished from the rest and I guessed that sheer poverty had driven them to respond to my offer.

'Which are free?'

'The first two.' Horatius clapped his hands and called, sharply. 'Claudia! Pholis! Take two steps forward!'

Pholis was short, stocky, her face and shoulders broad. Her arms were almost as thick as my own. Pushing back her hair I studied her face. It was hard, weathered, older than it should have been.

'Why do you want to fight in the arena?'

'I had a husband and son and together we worked a small farm. Both are dead now. I've worked for years to stay alive and I figure that I can't lose. If I'm killed, it's over. If I win, then I'm free of the land.'

'Strong?'

'Test me.' She held out her hand and I gripped it. Her fingers, thick and hard, pressed like iron.

'You?'

Claudia was taller, more graceful, younger, but with a hard directness about her eyes.

'I'm barren and my husband divorced me. For me now it's a choice between the arena and a brothel—and I prefer the arena.'

There was no point in questioning the others. Slaves, they were here because their masters had ordered them to be. Slowly I walked down the line. One was unable to stop coughing, another had a swollen belly, either she was pregnant or had some form of dropsy, a third had eyes filmed with cataracts, a fourth had a neck bulging with goitre.

Dismissed, they returned to their masters as, again, I examined the rest. One had eyes like a pleading animal.

'Master!' she said quickly. 'I have a small child. A baby still at my breast. If we are parted—'

'Fall out. You are unsuitable.' I added, in a whisper, 'Say nothing as to why I've rejected you.'

Behind me Horatius cleared his throat.

'The one on the right, Atilus,' he said quietly. 'She was to have been married. A local artisan intends to buy her and set her free.'

She joined the discards at my signal. To the four slaves remaining I said, 'Strip. You other two also. All of you, strip.'

Naked they looked a poor bunch in the clear sunlight, yet all had prominent breasts, unmistakable hips, and I could spot no deformities. Washed, oiled, fed, and trained, they would have to do.

Putting Pholis and Claudia in charge I had them dress and go to the baths; after to eat and be fitted with sandals and more respectable clothing. Horatius, who helped me to settle with the owners, beating down their price and arranging a kickback, beamed as I slipped a few gold coins into his palm.

'Atilus, you're generous, and that's what I like about gladiators. Easy come and easy go, as they say. I remember one time, about two years ago now, it must be, when I'd arranged a small *munera*. Sixteen pairs together with beasts and the usual acrobats. Only a small show but a good one, though I say it myself. There was a Thracian who was like quicksilver, he was so fast. He fought in the morning, at noon, and again in the afternoon. The betting went wild, some wanting the good odds offered against his opponents, others trying to play it safe. Well, the last fight was fixed and I'll admit it. The Thracian was to fall and the editor would give him life. He did too, though it was a near thing what with the losers all yelling for his blood. Anyway, afterwards the Thracian, who'd made quite a pile, stood some of us dinner. All the food you could imagine and a sea of wine.'

Musingly he clinked the coins.

'Maybe something like that could be arranged if you were to stay for a while. In ten days I've to put on a three-day *munera*. Interested?'

'I've got to get these women back to Rome.'

'I'd forgotten.' Horatius shrugged. 'From what I've seen of them you could be wasting your time. One cut and they'll run.

It's obvious that the owners only sold what rubbish they could spare. Still, you know what you're doing.'

'And if you hear of any really good talent...?'

'I'll let you know,' he promised. 'And I'll pass the word among visiting *lanistae*. Well, Atilus, good luck. It's my guess you'll need it.'

Before leaving town I paid a last visit to the *duumvir*. It was one I could have done without, but it would have been discourteous to have left without making my farewells and I could need his help another time.

Aquinus Rebilus was affable. 'Well, young man, I hope that I've been of service to you and to the Emperor.'

'I couldn't have done without you.'

'Got what you came for, eh?' He puffed out his cheeks. 'Can't say that I see the sense of it myself, but then, I'm old-fashioned. All these new ideas baffle me. Once you get women into the arena, who knows what might happen? They might even start thinking they are the equal of men.' The concept amused him so much that he burst into laughter. 'Ridiculous, of course,' he said wiping his eyes. 'Imagine women serving in the legions! Female senators! Women physicians!' He shook his head and grunted when I mentioned his daughter. 'Natalia? She's out somewhere.'

'Give her my regards and your lady too,' I said. 'If ever you're in Rome, don't hesitate to call on me.'

'I won't. And the Emperor? You'll—'

'I'll mention you by name,' I promised. 'Now, if you will excuse me, I must be on my way.'

I caught up with the others about a mile down the road and trotted gently behind them. They walked as I'd expected, shoulders drooping, eyes down, their attitude that of cattle going to slaughter. Even the free women who should have known better had unconsciously adopted the attributes of the others.

Halting them I said, 'Now listen to me. You are women, but I want you to start acting and thinking like men. Like fighters. To survive in the arena you need training, fitness, and an attitude of mind. The first two I can give you, and I will teach you the third. You slaves remember this, you'll be fighting for your freedom. You will all be fed, clothed, taken care of if you are hurt. You'll have money and prestige, but you have to earn them. We haven't much time, so your training will start immediately. You'll keep your shoulders back, your chests forward, your heads up, and your eyes off the road. You'll march, not slouch. You understand?'

Pholis said, 'We're not soldiers.'

'If you want to stay with me, you'll do as I say. If not, you can quit now.' I waited a moment but she made no move. 'At the next town, you'll swear to a contract. It'll bind you to me for a year. You've got a day to think it over. Now move!'

I pressed them hard, but not so hard as to numb them with weariness. Yet it wasn't merciful to be kind. Their muscles had to be strengthened, their body-tone raised, unaccustomed disciplines established. Three times a day they ate good, wholesome food, the largest meal being at night when I gave them a ration of wine. Both of the free women signed contracts at the end of the first day. By the time we reached Rome all were marching like legionaires.

CHAPTER THIRTEEN

I woke to a shriek of rage and wearily rolled from my bed. It was barely dawn, a pale light illuminating my chamber, a thin mist outside the window softening the outlines of the practice ground. Yawning I slipped into tunic and sandals. Looking back, it seemed that I hadn't had a decent night's rest since my return from Perusia a month ago. Always there was something; an amorous matron whom it would be impolitic to refuse, a young knight eager to talk until the small hours, a fight among the women.

This time it was Claudia. She stood at the side of her bed screaming at Pholis and accusing her of having stolen her comb. Pholis had a different explanation for her roommate's anger.

'She wanted to get into bed with me and I wouldn't let her.'

'You liar!' Claudia lunged towards the other woman, her fingers hooked to tear at the eyes. Catching her, I held her fast despite her struggles. 'Look at the ugly cow!' she stormed. 'Who'd want to get close to her? I'm not that desperate.'

'Calm down.' She was naked under a thin nightgown which barely reached her knees and I slapped her hard on the buttocks. 'Stop it or I'll have you whipped.'

'She'd like that,' sneered Pholis. 'The bitch is a pervert.'

'Me a pervert! What about you? The things you do to yourself are disgusting!'

'Shut up, the pair of you!' There could have been truth in Pholis' accusation. Claudia hadn't flinched from my slap, instead she pressed herself hard against me. Tiredly, I pushed her away.

'If there's any more of this nonsense I'll have you both punished,' I said harshly. 'I've had enough of these squabbles. If it isn't you, then it's some of the others. Now you've woken the rest. The pair of you get to the kitchens and help to prepare the morning meal.'

'We aren't slaves,' protested Claudia. 'It isn't our job.'

Without hesitation I slapped her hard across the face.

'You'll do as I say and like it. It's time you women learned discipline. Argue with me again, and I'll have you scourged until the flesh is torn from your spine. Now move, the pair of you!'

I was angry and it showed. Claudia looked at me, blanching, the red welts of my fingers stark against her cheek. Then, demurely, she followed Pholis from the room.

Over our meal of barley Agonestes smiled when I told him of the incident.

'You're learning what I've known for years, Atilus. Women are more trouble than they're worth. But what's happened is your own fault. You've been too gentle.'

He was right, but I'd been soft for a reason. To treat slaves like animals, to beat and cow them and to break their spirit, was no way to prepare them for the arena. I wanted them to be fighters, and to achieve that I had first to build them up and to instil a sense of personal awareness. Good food, regular exercise, and rest had changed them all for the better.

Now they were becoming restive.

Had they been men, a regular supply of women would have eased their tensions; sexual favours granted for strict obedience. But they were not men, and to supply them with partners was to risk unwanted pregnancies. Associations had been formed among themselves, that I knew, but lesbian involvements held other dangers, jealousy for one.

'Work them,' suggested Agonestes. 'Wear them down. Make them so tired they will fall asleep as soon as their heads hit the pillow. That'll take the juice out of them, and they're ready for some real, hard training.'

Later, looking at them on the practice ground, I had to agree.

Aside from the half-dozen I had brought back with me from Perusia, another fourteen trotted, stooped, and stretched in the sun. Some Agonestes had bought while I'd been away, others had arrived as the word had passed, and now a score of women had to be trained. One in particular held my attention.

She was almost as tall as myself, blonde, her shoulders and hips wide. Her skin held a milky whiteness, and her eyes, deep-set, were a clear blue. Her breasts were large, widely spaced, firm and high on her chest. Her face was broad, strongly boned, the chin firm and the lips full. A German who had almost killed her master when he'd tried to rape her. A recalcitrant slave whom he had sold to me in revenge.

Now she stood listlessly swinging a heavy practice sword at a straw-wrapped post.

'Verdalia!' I stepped towards her and stood at her side. 'That's no way to use a sword. Hit, girl! Slam it home with all the strength you've got. I want to see that straw fly like chaff.'

The sword fell as lightly as before.

'Verdalia! Look at me!' Sullenly she obeyed. 'Do you know why you are here, girl?'

'Because I had no choice.'

'You're here to be trained to fight. I am going to train you. Now you have a choice: either you obey me or you will be punished. If you disobey, you will be whipped. If you attempt any physical violence on any of the staff, you will be crucified. Do you understand?'

I had spoken loudly with intent and could sense the hushed attention of the others.

'Now hit it, girl! Hit!'

I carried a whip dangling from my right wrist. A short-braided thong attached to a heavy stock. Now, as again she barely touched the straw, I lifted it and cut her across the buttocks.

'Hit!' Again the lash fell. 'Hit!' A third time. 'Hit it, blast you! Hit!'

For a moment I was afraid she would disobey, and then chopped straw flew like chaff as she slammed the blade at the post. For her, perhaps, it held my face and figure, her savage blows the result of a furious, personal hatred, but I didn't care. She had obeyed.

Agonestes pursed his lips as I rejoined him. 'A hard one, Atilus, but possibly the best we have. Let's hope you don't have to break her.'

A hope I shared. The woman attracted me in a way I found disturbing. It had been hard to apply the whip, harder still to refrain from touching the smooth bloom of her skin. And, when she had looked at me, I hadn't liked what I'd seen in her eyes.

'Fit up an awning,' I said. 'Have her practice in the shade. I don't want to spoil the whiteness of her skin.'

For a moment Agonestes looked at me then he said, 'The others? Shall we sort them out now?'

As yet all had received the same training designed to build muscle and develop speed and dexterity. The time had been far too short to accomplish very much, but the women would not be set against experienced gladiators, but only against each other. Even so, they would have to put on a good show or they would be jeered from the arena and my reputation tarnished with Nero.

I had decided to form them into two groups and there was method in my choice. Those who had the largest and firmest breasts would use the net and trident on the basis that, as *retiarii*, they would expose the maximum amount of flesh to the avid eyes of the crowd. Those not so well endowed would use the equipment of a *secutor*, the latticed helmet hiding unattractive features.

Training them as Thracians would have exposed more flesh, but the small round shield, the open helmet, and the curved blade would have made them too vulnerable, poorly trained as they would be.

Pholis was chosen to be a *secutar*. Claudia a *retiarius*, together with three lithe Nubians, a leggy Greek, and two others who were both slim and attractive. Looking at Verdalia, I hesitated. Her white skin would make a fine display and her magnificent body shown to the best advantage if she used the net. And, as a *retiarius*, she would have the odds in her favour. The last decided me to include her with the others.

Agonestes nodded at my choice. 'You've picked well, Atilus. I'll keep her in the shade. We each teach our own?'

'Yes.'

Telling the women of their respective roles, I had them stand in a circle as the Greek and I gave a demonstration fight. We made it simple, accentuating each movement, slowing the action to make it clear what we did and why we did it. Then, with the women fitted out with practice equipment, we set to work.

It was hard going. Agonestes had the easier task, finding the women quickly learned how to cast the net, even though slow on learning to handle the trident, but my group of a dozen were pathetically clumsy. As the days slid into weeks my temper became shorter and shorter.

'No, Pholis! No!' I thrust between her and her opponent. 'The shield is for defence, you hold it close to your body—so! You don't lift it and wave it each time you're attacked.'

Until they had become proficient, I was setting one *secutar* against the other, knowing that it was useless to have them face the net unless they could handle their arms. Also, later, they might have to fight against each other sword to sword. Something no two *retiarii* ever did.

Tiredness had made her short. 'You lift your shield,' she snapped. 'I've seen you.'

A child teaching its grandmother to suck eggs. With difficulty I held my scathing reply.

'Let me demonstrate.' I faced her, poised and ready. 'Ready! Right, strike!'

She swung a vicious blow at my shield and I struck back in turn. As I'd expected, her shield lifted as she automatically tried to ward off the blow. Immediately I ran my sword over the surface, under the lower edge and, lifting it, jabbed the blunted point hard against her stomach.

'See?'

Gasping, for I had deliberately not been gentle, she said, 'That was a trick.'

'No. A natural attack against a poor defence.'

'But what could I have done?'

'I'll show you. Now do the same thing to me.'

This time I struck first, a light blow, and then, as she cut back, lifted my shield as she had done. Her reaction was slow but she managed to get her sword down and under. As she thrust I swayed to my right and clamped my shield hard against her arm, trapping her wrist and sword between my elbow and side. Before she could do anything I'd brought my own blade up to rest the edge against the unprotected inside of her bicep.

'A cut now and you'd be crippled.'

'Another trick.'

'No, training.'

'What could I have done?'

'Anything rather than just stand there like a stuffed owl.' I was savagely harsh; she had done her best but others were listening. 'You could have thrown your shield across your body between us. You could have moved to your left and dragged free your arm, not forgetting to turn your blade so the edge would cut. You could have tried to knee me in the groin, or screamed, or—'

'Screamed?'

'Why not? It might have startled your opponent and given you a chance.' Stepping back, I raised my voice. 'Listen, all of you. This isn't a game. You go into the arena to kill or be killed, and how you kill isn't as important as staying alive. The crowd might laugh or they might jeer—but you'll be the one walking to the Gate of Life while the other is dragged through the Gate of Death. How you leave the sand is up to you—but one way you use only once.'

Words which I felt had little meaning, and I said so to Agonestes one night as we sat yawning over wine. The days were too long and the work too hard for the two of us, and yet

I'd been unable to get useful help. Good instructors were too conscious of their dignity to handle women, and the rest were more interested in using their whips than teaching their indifferent skills.

Even the guards were a problem. Three times I'd dismissed men who had ventured where they shouldn't. The fourth time, when finding a man trying to break into the room where Verdalia slept, I'd pulped his nose, and would have beaten him to death if Heraculis hadn't stopped me.

The example had prevented further breaches of discipline, but I felt as if I were living on the edge of a volcano.

'Relax, Atilus.' Agonestes poured me more wine. 'You walk about with a face like that of a savage animal. One thing, though, it keeps the women in line. Some of them are afraid to breathe when you're around.'

'Verdalia?'

We were drinking from silver goblets, the gift of his patron and now, as Agonestes drank, he looked at me steadily over the rim.

'She's on your mind, isn't she?'

'I think about her at times, yes,' I admitted. 'But no more than the others.'

'I've never known you to lie, Atilus,' he said gently. 'So why start now? I've seen how you look at her and, if we were lovers, I would be jealous.'

'Nonsense!'

'Perhaps.' His shrug was expressive of his disbelief. 'I hope that it is, but I don't think so. And I'm not the only one who has noticed. Claudia, Syrenne, even Pholis has mentioned it. They think Verdalia is your favourite, and that you have put her in a room alone in order to visit her at night.'

'A lie.'

'That I know. Perhaps it would help if you did. The woman is consumed with hate. It ruins her concentration and makes her too open to anyone who knows how to handle a sword.' Agonestes shook his head at my expression. 'I'm sorry, Atilus, but you have to know the truth. She could be the best we have, but she lacks something. The urge to kill, to survive no matter what the cost. I've seen it before. A captive can be eaten with hatred, but it turns inward against himself. He is sullen, recalcitrant, practically inviting death because, by dying, he thinks that he is defeating Rome.'

'And the rest?'

'All of them lack fire. They learn under the threat of the whip but they are mechanical. Of my group there isn't one who could stand up to a *tiro* for more than a few minutes and yours is little better. If Nero wants to get a laugh at their expense they will give it to him.'

With their blood and pain and death accompanying the derisive mirth of the crowd. And Agonestes was right, as I knew. A condemnation echoed by Cadius Publius the next day.

He arrived late in the afternoon accompanied by a sleek body-servant who sniffed disdainfully at the house and the furnishings it contained. A slave who regarded himself as in a special class for reasons which I could guess. Cadius himself was affable, extending his hand, gripping my forearm as I returned the salutation.

'Atilus, it is good to see you again. You have no objection to my visiting you?'

'None.'

'I have been away or would have come before. All Rome is engrossed with your venture. The Emperor himself spoke of it only the other day. It was at a musical evening to which he invited a few, close friends, and he was in superb voice.'

A neat way of telling me that he was strong in Nero's favour.

'And Ricilia Rubinia?'

'A fine woman and so understanding. She is with her husband in Campania.' Cadius dismissed the past with an elegant gesture. 'Now, if I may see your school?'

Summoning Heraculis to take care of his slave, I led the young man over the house, showing him the rooms in which the women slept, the kitchens, the baths, finally leading him into the sunlight of the practice ground. Agonestes was hard at work, Verdalia prominent among those he was teaching, her hair a blaze of gold as, like a marionette, she handled net and trident.

'A fine woman,' mused Cadius. 'But, surely, a little stiff?'

'The normal training of a gladiator takes two years,' I reminded him. 'We have had these women only a matter of weeks.'

'Of course, and you have done marvels, and yet—' He broke off, shrugging.

'You find them lacking?'

'My dear, Atilus, who am I to denigrate what you have accomplished? And yet I have some small knowledge of the arena, as you must agree. Yet I am sure that, given time, they will improve.'

'Naturally.'

'If,' he said blandly, 'they are given the time.'

His tone held an odd note which gave rise to questions, but Agonestes came to join us before I could ask them. He was sweating, dust traced with thin rivulets on his naked torso. Cadius smiled as I made the introductions and, as their eyes met, I sensed something pass between them, a recognition, an understanding, and was not surprised when they moved off to study the *secutares* at their drill.

Time!

Had there been a hint, a warning? There had been unrest in the city, a statue of Poppaea overthrown and crowds chanting Octavia's name. Garlands had adorned her statues, and the taverns were full of rumours that Nero wanted to divorce his wife and marry Poppaea. A diversion would help to calm the public and I could guess what it would be.

But the women were far from ready. To make them fight would be a pathetic slaughter.

Irritably I strode to where the *retiarii* stood as Agonestes had left them. A few toyed with their nets or poised their tridents but, looking at them through Cadius's eyes, I could see how wooden they were.

'You!' I pointed at Verdalia. 'Come at me!'

I had no shield or sword but neither was necessary. A sweep of my left arm flung aside the net, another with my right pushed away the trident.

'Again!'

She was slow, indifferent, not even trying to improve. My anger mounted as, conscious of Cadius watching, I checked her efforts to snare and stab me.

'Pholis! Come over here!' I pointed at Verdalia as she ran to obey. 'Now the pair of you fight and put your minds on the job. Move!'

A cut of my whip sent Pholis into action. Verdalia backed, lifted the net, cast it far to one side. Steel clashed as she parried the sword with her trident but, again, she was slow.

My whip cracked across her buttocks.

'Faster! Watch what you are doing! Keep at it until I tell you to stop!'

I turned, took three steps, then heard Agonestes' warning shout. Spinning I saw the flash of sunlight from blonde hair, saw a face distorted into an animal-like snarl, caught the dull gleam of tines as she thrust the trident directly at my eyes.

Blunt though the points and edges were, they could still blind and kill if driven hard enough. And she intended to kill.

My right hand rose with a volition of its own. I felt the slap of the wooden shaft against my palm, the vicious strength she had put into the thrust, then the points had lifted to rip through my hair. As Verdalia came stumbling towards me, I kicked her just below the ribs.

Winded, she doubled to fall and roll gasping on the dirt.

'Atilus!' Agonestes came running towards me, Cadius close behind, 'Are you hurt?'

A tine had ripped my scalp, sending blood to run down my forehead and into my eyes. Wiping it away, I looked at the carmine smears, then at the girl where she lay writhing on the ground.

'Atilus?' Agonestes looked at me, a question in his eyes.

'Let her lie where she is until she recovers.'

'And then?'

'Crucify her!'

CHAPTER FOURTEEN

It was late when I retired but I found it impossible to sleep. Rising I stepped towards the window and stared down at the practice ground below. The moon was full and high, obscured at times by patches of scudding cloud, and the leaves of the laurels and fig trees made an uneasy rustling as they were stirred by a soft breeze from the west.

On the ground the shadow of the cross lay stark and clear, its burden a formless blur.

Formless and soundless. Even while guards had lifted and held her for Agonestes to lash her extended wrists to the cross-piece, Verdalia had remained silent.

Testing the bindings, he had snapped at the guard busy fitting the block beneath her naked feet.

'Higher!'

'But—'

'Higher!'

The higher the block, the less would be the constriction on her chest, the less savage the cramps. The man had looked at me, had seen my face, had obeyed the Greek without further argument.

Nor had Cadius argued when I had bidden him a brief fare-well. He would have liked to linger, to watch the woman in her pain, but he had left together with his slave, no doubt to spread word of the harsh discipline and savage treatment I meted to those who defied my rule.

The rest of the day had been spent in arduous exercise, whip and tongue lashing the women to greater efforts, the grim presence of the cross a warning to all.

I tensed as something seemed to move below, then relaxed as I realised that it was only the shadow cast by the shifting of leaves. The guards were discreetly hidden or on patrol outside the walls. Only from below came a faint whisper of noise; women restless in their sleep or finding relief from tension in their own way. A cough, a rustle, a soft creaking, the gasp of eased passion, a muttered cry born of tormented dreams. Small, normal sounds which I barely heard.

Dressing, I moved to the door. Moonlight threw a ghostly radiance which illuminated the passages, and I moved along them, checking barred doors. All seemed as it should be, but something had changed. Now the atmosphere was more familiar than it had been. Punishment, decided and inflicted, had added a thin edge of steel. The example which had been made threw an invisible miasma over the house and grounds, the shadow of the crucified woman extending even into the cells.

Outside the air was cool, carrying a thin tang of brine, the scent of fecund vegetation. Again I thought I saw movement, a shadow which seemed to poise and then vanish as I stepped towards it. Another trick of the light or an illusion created by sharpened suspicion. A man would have been left to suffer in isolation, but a woman would provide tempting bait for the guards. A helpless morsel to touch and to fondle, unable to resist the thrust of hungry fingers.

Stealthily I made a circuit of the area, finding nothing, halting at last before the cross.

'Verdalia?'

She hung as though dead, her head tilted a little to one side, her face turned so that I could only see her profile. Sweat dewed her skin and her lips were tightly drawn over her teeth. Dark stains of blood showed over her chin, more blood showing on her palms where she had driven her nails into the flesh. The calves above her bare feet where they rested on the block were tense, the muscles showing rigid beneath the skin.

I touched them, running my hands up over her knees, the pronounced curve of her thighs, halting as I reached the lower edge of the single garment which covered her nakedness. It reached midway down her thighs, leaving her arms and neck bare, the swell of hips and breasts prominent beneath the fabric.

'Verdalia?'

Again she made no response to my whisper, though beneath my fingers I could feel a muscle jerk and quiver. The cross was low and the juncture of her legs was on a level with my face. For a moment the urge to close the distance between us, to press my lips against her, to kiss, to caress, was almost overwhelming.

'Verdalia!'

This time she stirred a little, her head falling so that her chin rested on her breast, her knees sagging so that the muscles of her arms bunched and knotted as they took the entire weight of her body.

Then she moaned, a sound dragged from the caverns of the damned.

A ladder lay to one side. I grabbed it, set it into place, my fingers tearing at the lashings of her wrists. They were looser than I had expected; Agonestes had been merciful.

He came running to join me as I thrust my way into the house and into Heraculis's room. His bed was wide and, I suspected, often held more than one, but now he was alone.

'Master! What's happened?'

'Move!' I dropped the girl on the vacated couch and ripped the garment from her body with a single jerk. 'Massage, quickly, she's knotted with cramps!'

Agonestes fetched warm oil and pads, one of which he placed over her mouth as she began to scream.

'No need to wake the others,' he explained. 'What made you go down?'

'I thought I saw someone. And you?'

'I was restless.' He didn't meet my eyes. 'I thought that, maybe a guard—' He broke off, not voicing the suspicion. 'Here, let me help.'

It took time and the night was dying before the last knotted muscles eased to our ministrations. After the first effort Verdalia made no effort to scream and lay panting, her eyes like brittle glass.

When I offered her wine she dashed the goblet from my hand. 'Roman pig!'

'Watch your tongue, girl!' said Heraculis sharply. 'Have you forgotten the cross so soon?'

'Did I put myself on it?'

'Yes.' He was curt. 'You were warned as were the others. Did you think it was a joke? You tried to kill your master before witnesses—what else could he have done?'

Sullen, she made no answer.

'Had you been a house-slave and had you succeeded in your murderous attempt, you and every other slave in the household would have been executed,' continued Heraculis. 'Here we are lucky in more ways than one, but the law isn't gentle. You would have stayed on the cross. Others would have joined you. I would have lost a good master and, perhaps, have been thrown to the beasts. It's time you learned to obey.'

'And become a fawning dog as you are?' She made no effort to hide her contempt. 'Kiss the boots of those who made you a slave. No wonder your country is so decadent. My people have more pride. They can kill me but they can never make me obey.'

'Don't talk like a fool!' Heraculis trembled in his anger. 'Have you ever been seared with red hot irons? Flogged until you stood in a puddle of your own blood? Watched as men have had the eyes gouged from their heads or the tongues ripped from their mouths? Have you ever known the inside of a mine?'

'Death comes only once.'

'Then die! Act the fool and die—but don't take me with you!'

'Who would want a slave who kisses his chains?'

'That's enough!' I gestured Heraculis from the room. 'He is an old man and has suffered more than you know. Was it kind to mock his pride?'

'Is Rome kind?'

'Rome has learned.' Agonestes had brought her a clean garment. Throwing it at her I said, 'Get dressed.'

'Aren't you going to rape me?' Her tone was ironic. 'One of you holding a dagger at my throat while the other takes his pleasure? Isn't that the Roman manner? Or will you summon others to help you? One to stand on my wrists while more open my legs. Romans! Filth! How else can you get your women?'

'Shut your mouth!'

'Why?' She reared upright on the bed, the garment ignored, warm lamplight glistening on her oiled skin. 'Think of it, Roman. Learn how you treat your captive women. That's how the legionaires taught my mother the grace and culture of Rome. That was after they had raided my village and burned it. After they had killed my father and brothers. After they had taken my little sister and smashed her head against a tree. Romans!' Her voice held an aching hatred. 'Would the gods grant me the power to kill you all!'

A feeling which I had once known and had, somehow, forgotten and yet, listening to her, I was again in the past, a boy of ten looking at the dead and ravished body of his mother. A woman with torn wrists and straddled legs, blood between her thighs and a dagger thrust in the heart. Murdered by the lustful legionaires of conquering Rome.

'Atilus!'' I felt the touch of Agonestes's hand on my shoulder, the quick urgency of his voice. 'Atilus—she didn't know.'

A girl, a German who lay on the bed, cringing now, her face startled, afraid of the emotion she saw on my own.

Thickly I said, 'I will tell you this only once. I am not a Roman. I am a Briton, a captive like yourself. Like you I have no reason to love Rome but, unlike you, I was determined to survive. Dead a man can do nothing. Rome is built on a mountain of dead. Would one body more make any difference?'

'You a captive? A slave?'

'No longer,' said Agonestes quietly. 'Now get dressed. Atilus, leave her and let's get some wine.'

I was shaking as I drank it, too conscious of his watchful

eyes, spilling a little down my tunic as I tilted the goblet.

As I set it down he said, 'Atilus, as your friend I should go in there and cut that woman's throat.'

'Why?'

'She is trouble and we both know it. I saw the way you looked at her and I know why you took her down from the cross.'

'The same reason you ran out with a sword in your hand?'

'No. I was protecting her for your sake. But you—Atilus, if you want the woman why don't you just take her? She might fight a little, but perhaps that is what she wants, to be mastered. Take her and forget her.' His eyes narrowed a little as I made no comment. 'You do want her, don't you?'

I remembered how she had felt beneath my hands, the way I had felt as my fingers and palms had massaged her body. The impact of her eyes, the sound of her voice, the ineffable fragrance of her femininity.

'Yes, I want her, but—'

'You want more than that,' he interrupted. 'You want her to want you. It isn't enough for you to simply take her. You want to feel her respond to your passion, to anticipate it and induce it with her own. My friend, I know too well how you feel, and I am sorry for you. It is never easy to be in love and for you, with her, it's hopeless.'

'Why?' I poured and drank more wine. 'Because she hates me?'

'She doesn't hate you. She may hate Rome but you aren't Rome and now she knows it. And she must know that you have been gentle with her. Gentle, not weak. A woman of her race would appreciate the difference and respect it.' The twin of the goblet I held stood on the table. Agonestes filled it, sipped and continued, quietly, 'Once you asked me how, if we were close, we could ever face each other in the arena. Now I'll ask you a question. If you and she became lovers, how could you send her out on the sand?'

'I wouldn't.'

'Atilus, you have no choice. You are an imperial agent and

she is an imperial slave. You bought her with Nero's money and she is his property to do with as he wants. You are training her to be a gladiator, to fight and to kill, to win or to die. And, knowing what you know, how long do you think she will last?'

Against one of the others long enough, but the show would be poor and the crowd would become impatient. Beasts could be turned loose against them or male gladiators sent to end the farce. And Agonestes had learned of another danger.

'Cadius Publius mentioned it,' he said. 'He and I have an affinity, as you may have noticed. We are to meet again and, when we do, I shall try to learn more. But it was obvious he had a purpose in coming here.'

I had assumed that it was to warn me of the shortage of available time for training, now I was not so sure. He could have come simply to look, to watch, and to learn.

'Exactly,' said Agonestes when I mentioned it. 'He was more than idly curious and I gained the impression that he wanted to check progress in order to gain information which would be of use in making future wagers. And he was too pleased at what he saw.'

'Which could mean that there is another troupe of women training to be gladiators.' My goblet slammed hard on the table. 'It's more than possible. Such a thing would appeal to Nero's sense of humour. He could even have known they were being trained when he made me an imperial agent.'

A joke which would result in pain and ignominious death as my own fighters fell beneath others, and I had no doubt they would fall. The essential fire was lacking, the determination I had been too gentle to instil. And as they died so would my own reputation go with them.

'No!' I strode across the room and stood looking at the far door behind which Verdalia rested. 'No!'

'They have to fight, Atilus.'

'Fight, yes, but be slaughtered? Those women haven't a chance against ruthless fighters and you know it. If there are other women gladiators, ours are beaten before they step on the sand. I've failed, Agonestes. I should have turned them into killers; instead, I'll be sending them to their deaths.'

'It isn't your fault, Atilus,' he protested. 'There's been no time and the material is poor. Aside from Pholis and Claudia, we're dealing with slaves and those two are little better.'

The truth, but it didn't help. 'I should have taught them.'

'How? With more beatings? The use of hot irons? Will that turn them into first-class fighters?'

'No. It has to come from inside. They have to feel it in every bone and muscle. We must give them the spirit, the hate, and resolve, the single-minded purpose to go in and win. And we haven't much time. How do we do it? How?'

'I don't know,' he said quietly. 'If I did the arena—'

'The arena!' I turned to face him. The obvious which we'd overlooked because it was too familiar. 'Of course, man, the arena. It's time they learned just what they're heading into. Let them see it, feel it, smell, and taste it. Show them the blood, the spilled guts, the wounds, the pain, and death.'

'And after?'

Set them one against the other with sharpened weapons, letting the dead teach the living, winnowing them down to a hardened few. Forget to be gentle. Forget they were women, naturally slow, naturally clumsy. Remember only that only the strong and ruthless could survive and hope, with the aid of the gods, that Verdalia would be among them.

CHAPTER FIFTEEN

For reasons of secrecy I took the women to a small amphi-theatre to the east of Rome. The *munera*, though only a one-day affair, promised to be interesting. The name written largest on the announcements was that of Rufus Pisanus, who wanted to make certain that all knew exactly who was meeting the expense of the games.

Leaving the women in the charge of Agonestes, I found an official who frowned as I told him what I wanted. A frown which turned into a smile as I showed him gold.

'A party of twenty-five and you want good seats. Well, I can't put you on the podium, but I can arrange something. Take them around to the gladiators entrance and I'll get you fixed up.'

The stench hit us as we stepped from the early morning sunlight into the shadowed gloom. I was accustomed to it, but I saw the women's expressions as they breathed air laden with pungent odours: sweat, blood, rancid grease all coupled with the reek of caged beasts.

Seated, I studied the programme I had bought. After the usual initial events came the high points of the *munera*, and the noted gladiators were listed so as to give a guide to those placing wagers.

Barbius Ner. IV. S v Sulpici Ner. III. R.
Menicus Gal. II. M v Gannicus. Gal. V. T.

Barbius was a *secutar* from the Neroniani school and had fought four times. He was to be matched against Sulpici who had been trained at the same school, a *retiarius* who had fought three times. Menicus was a *myrmillo* from the Gallic school and would fight Gannicus a Thracian. He also was from the Gallic school, but while Gannicus had fought five times, Menicus had only fought twice. Unless Gannicus had been matched well beyond his class, his experience would make him a sure winner. Yet things were not always what they seemed, and a Thracian was at a disadvantage when opposed to a *myrmillo*. He had speed on his side but that was about all.

Agonestes, seated on the tier behind me, leaned forward. We, together with three guards, had accompanied the women. He also had a programme.

'Atilus, I've heard of Menicus and he's good. His trainer has been nursing him and he could be due to win. Five gold pieces?'

'Make it ten. And Sulpici?'

'An even match as far as I can see. Best to wait until they come on the sand.'

We had brought food and wine in baskets and took the chance to eat before the crowd were admitted. When they were, they streamed into the amphitheatre like a horde of ants. Some of the patricians had also arrived, taking their places on the podium and lower tiers. Both men and women were elegantly dressed and affected a bored disdain. A façade which would quickly dissolve when the action began.

A blast of trumpets announced the procession. First came the holder of the games. Rufus Pisanus was a big man, his face wreathed with smiles as, riding in his chariot, he circled the arena three times before taking his place on the podium in the editor's chair.

With the editor had come musicians, who continued playing as the rest of the procession streamed into the arena. In the city itself, especially if the Emperor had attended the games, there would have been Vestal Virgins, a long series of items including the statues of gods, scenes from classical Greece, tableaux presented by the various guilds, but here the Master of Games had concentrated less on empty spectacle than on getting down to the real business.

Not that spectacle was lacking. A riot of colour flowed over and around the arena, brilliant reds and greens, yellows and blues, gold and silver flashing as acrobats turned and tumbled, jugglers threw balls and plates high, catching them with amazing dexterity, maidens with sweet voices waving fronds of laurel and fern in time to the music, slaves hauling the wheeled cages which contained snarling beasts.

But, as always, the gladiators with their glinting weapons and armour, their crested helmets, their cloaks, their proud arrogance, provided the high point of the procession.

As they filed out, the roar of their salute still ringing in my ears, I glanced at the women. They were seated to either side, others on the upper tier, and already the holiday atmosphere had gripped them as it had the crowd.

Even Verdalia seemed to be relaxed though, as she saw me looking at her, her face stiffened into a hostile mask.

'Watch,' I told her. 'Concentrate on what is coming next.'

'Why?'

'You'll know when it happens, and remember, you could be down there on the sand.'

Rufus Pisanus, unlike many editors, knew his business and he had a good Master of Games handling his show. No further time was wasted in preliminaries. As we watched a group of men and women, some of them barely girls, were pushed through the Gate of Life into the arena. The men were dressed in skins, the legs tied so that they couldn't stand upright and had to move in little hops which looked ridiculous and amused the crowd. The women and girls were naked aside from a strip of thin fabric about their hips. Their breasts were stained and gilded, the nipples reflecting the sun like stars caught in a field of crimson.

Verdalia looked at me, frowning.

'They are *trinqui*,' I explained. 'Sacrificial victims condemned by the courts or sold by their owners as useless or recalcitrant. In the old days they were used to appease the gods, and the crowd likes to think they are still used for that purpose.'

'And?'

'Watch.'

With a soft grate of wood, doors slid upwards in openings around the arena. From one of them came a tiger, snarling, turning to look at the fire which had seared its rear and driven it from its cage. Others followed, striped and expensive beasts, caught and transported from a distant land. A dozen of them, bewildered, savage, ready to kill.

They circled the group of pathetic victims, tails lashing, bellies low, claws raking the sand. Then one of the girls, terrified, ran towards the editor where he sat on the podium, arms outstretched in an appeal for mercy.

'Master! Please!'

The crimson staining her breasts was blood, daubed on her flesh by a slave who had obtained it from a slaughtered chicken. Scenting it, a tiger loped over the sand towards the terrified girl. Trying to run she tripped and fell and before she could regain her feet the beast was on her. A swipe with its paw and her face was a tattered ruin of ripped and bleeding flesh, teeth bared to the sun, one eye hanging from its socket.

Her shriek of agony died as its jaws closed over her head.

As if at a signal, the other animals closed in. A man, desperately hopping, had one arm ripped from its socket and a fountain of blood gushed from the wound to dapple the sand as, still hopping, he hit the wall to rebound, to turn, and scream as claws tore out his guts.

A pattern repeated again and again as men and women ran and fell to roll and bleed, to scream and die, torn, bitten and ripped by fang and claw.

'Watch!' Verdalia had closed her eyes against the carnage and sat in horrified immobility. She rocked to the impact of my hand. 'Watch, I said! Watch!'

Others needed no urging. From all sides came the roar of

the crowd, laughter mingled with the hysterical shrieks induced by the sight of blood. Sounds born of pleasure and blood-lust, having nothing to do with pity or revulsion. To a Roman crowd those words had no meaning.

Men followed the beasts into the arena. *Bestiarii* trained and skilful and armed with swords. Crouching, weaving, they fought the tigers as if they had been men, stabbing, slashing, dodging. A display of courage which the crowd appreciated, though not as much as they relished the combat of men against men. Those who fought animals were not in the true gladiatorial class. They had their own schools and their own organisation and customs. Those who fell were dragged away and had a chance to live despite their failure if their wounds were not too serious.

'Atilus!' I felt a hand grip my thigh, the fingers mounting to my groin. Claudia, her face avid, stared at the scene below. A true Roman, she was one with the crowd.

Some of the others also, the Nubians, Pholis, the leggy girl from Greece. Others, like Verdalia, sat pale and looked ill. As the *bestiarii* left the arena and slaves ran to remove the bodies and to rake sand over the blood, entrails and mess, I fed them a little wine.

Verdalia pushed it away.

'No,' she said. 'I don't want it.'

'Drink. It will help.' I pushed the goblet against her lips. 'Drink, I say!'

'And, if I refuse to obey you, my master, will you send me to join those poor devils we saw torn apart by beasts?'

She was bold in her defiance. Too bold and only with an effort did I hold my temper. Why couldn't she understand?

'Listen,' I said. 'I'm trying to show you what it's all about. Like it or not, you're a part of the arena. Refuse to fight and you know now what will happen to you. Will your death hurt Rome? Do you want to die with the sound of derision in your ears? Is that the ambition of a woman of a warrior race?'

I had touched her; I could tell by the sudden clenching of her hands, and when next I offered her wine she did not refuse.

Trumpets announced the next event. The two pairs of *pugiles* ran into the arena, their hands bound with the *caestus*, leather straps studded with murderous spikes. As the boxers took up their stance the crowd hushed a little. This, if not exactly what they loved the most, offered a certain skill.

All of them were strong, bulky men, faces, torsos, and arms bearing old scars. The trick was to dodge, to hit, to block return blows. One went down within the first five minutes, his temple crushed, his cheek torn, lips split, and teeth shattered. Even as he sagged his opponent moved in, hammer-blows smashing ribs, splintering the jaw, turning one eye into a carmine jelly. A charonian finished the destruction with a blow from his hammer as Rufus Pisanus, obeying the will of the crowd, casually turned down his thumb.

The other pair, more evenly matched, slugged it out until both were exhausted. The combat was declared *stans missus*, a draw.

Some *andabatae* followed, men wearing closed helmets and armed with swords. Blinded, they were guided towards each other by slaves holding forked poles, slashing at the air or at imagined sounds. A turn designed to give comic relief, and one enjoyed by the crowd who roared with laughter and yelled advice and instruction. The laughter became hysterical as one, with a lucky cut, slashed the genitals from the other.

Bleeding to death, the unfortunate man rushed forward, took another cut on his left arm and managed to hack his opponent's leg behind the knee. Both, splashed with blood from head to foot, finally fell to be dispatched by the charonian.

An interval was called, vendors busy moving along the tiers selling wine and cakes as music played and a troupe of nimble girls performed an elaborate dance. After them came the distribution of lots, men throwing marked plaques into the rows, each of which entitled the holder to a prize. The gifts varied, sometimes a bag of coins, a valuable ring, parcels of spices, hampers of food and, according to the humour of the editor, sometimes yielding a package of dung, a sheaf of straw, or male genitals severed from a beast.

Other gifts were bestowed: cooked chickens, bread, jars of honey, cakes spiced and coated with crushed nuts, fish baked in vine leaves, small skins of wine. One of the women managed to snatch a chicken and shared it among those sitting beside her. To the others I issued the last of the food we had brought with us.

It was now past noon and the heat was becoming oppressive despite the awnings which shielded us from the direct glare of the sun. On the podium slaves threw incense into braziers and sprayed the air with perfume to sweeten the stench of blood.

Trumpets announced the recommencement of the events and, like a feral beast, the crowd settled in eager anticipation.

A group of gladiators ran from the Gate of Life and saluted the editor. Dressed in actual armour, they carried wooden swords. *Tiros*, the *lusorii* were there to gain a little experience and to pave the way for the real action to come. Judging the mood of the crowd with expert skill, the Master of Games allowed them to fight until just before they grew boring, the *tubae* ending the display with a blast of deep, commanding notes.

The *lusiones* over, now came the testing of weapons to ensure they were sharp. Slaves carried them to Rufus Pisanus who nodded his satisfaction. Again the trumpets and, as men ran to take up positions on the sand, the real purpose of the games commenced.

They started with some *dimachaeri*, men who fought almost naked with a long, sword-like dagger in each hand. An event designed to please the cognoscenti who affected a critical interest in the display of skill. Three pairs fought, all young and lithe, moving like dancers as they cut, backed, darted in to cut again, metal ringing as blade parried blade, thin streaks of red appearing on arms and torsos, blood running over the gleaning, sweat-covered skin.

One fell, dead before he hit the sand. The other two losers, one badly wounded, were given life and declared *missus*. They had lost but would live to fight again. A merciful verdict, and I suspected that some arrangement had been made by their *lanista* with the editor. Such fighters were not cheap, and the most generous giver of games liked to cut expenses if he could.

'Bad,' whispered Agonestes in my ear. 'If the women think they can fall and get away with it they won't go all out.'

'They'll learn,' I said grimly. 'The crowd won't stand for much more softness.'

The next bout proved it. Menicus and Gannicus came on next, out of turn, but such alterations were normal. The betting had been heavy and attention was concentrated on the two men. Trainers accompanied them together with slaves, but neither needed the lash of straps or the searing touch of hot irons to spur them on. The Thracian, lighter, moved to the attack, his curved sica catching and reflecting the sunlight as it lifted to fall, to cut and slash, to ring as it impacted the shield and sword of the *myrmillo*.

Menicus, the less experienced of the two, was cautious, but I liked the way he handled his shield. He was deft with his sword, too, not wasting energy in wild cuts but favouring the point. Twice the Thracian blocked with his shield; the third time, deluded by a feint, he was a little slow and, as one man, the crowd roared as blood spurted from his side.

'Habet!'

The yells increased as the Thracian, taking a chance, moved in and sent the curved edge of his weapon slicing at the face under the *myrmillo*'s helmet. Menicus backed in time, the tip laying open his cheek, then his sword darted forward to rip a long furrow over the other's chest.

Like the stab in the side the wound was relatively minor, but both cost the man a deal of blood, and such wounds, accumulating, could cripple and weaken. Shaken, Gannicus backed, crouching, his feet probing the sand as he watched for an opening.

A mistake. He should have ignored the wound, moved in, blocked the sword, and aimed for the eyes. An easy judgement to make when safe in the stands, not so easy when in the arena.

'Get in, Menacus!' screamed Claudia. 'Kill! Kill!'

Her body pressed close to mine and I could feel the sensual

heat of her flesh. Her eyes were wide, glazed, and her mouth gaped as she shrieked. A woman affected by the sight of blood and pain, stimulated sexually so that her hands clutched at her breasts. She was not alone. A few seats down a woman writhed against the hand a man had thrust under her garment. Another, to one side, gasped as she reached her orgasm.

Glancing at Verdalia, I saw a thin film of sweat on her upper lip, the whiteness of her teeth as they dug into the lower.

'*Iugula!*' screamed the crowd. 'Kill!'

Menacus needed no urging. He rushed at the other man like a storm, his brute strength beating down the weakened opposition. For a moment Gannicus fought back, blades clashing, the rasp of steel gliding over steel loud in the hushed expectancy. With the fury of desperation he managed to gain another hit, a slash on the *myrmillo*'s upper torso which was little more than a scratch. Then Menacus slammed aside the sica with his shield, blood spurting as his sword reached the Thracian's left bicep. A shrewd blow delivered with tremendous force, the edge chopping through the skin, muscle, the bone to sever the arm and to send it and the shield to fall on the sand.

Defenceless, blood jetting from the stump, Gannicus fell to throw aside his sica and to lift his hand, the forefinger raised in a plea for mercy.

Waving a handkerchief a man yelled, '*Mitte!* Send him away!'

The signal for his wish that mercy should be shown, but he was almost alone. A few others fluttered handkerchiefs and echoed his cry but the rest demanded death with a display of down-thrusting thumbs.

A signal repeated by the editor.

For a moment Manicus stood poised and then, with a quick thrust, sent his sword into the fallen man's heart.

As slaves came running to rake the sand and the dead man was dragged away I said, to Verdalia, 'You see? No one can be certain of receiving mercy in the arena. It's kill or be killed.'

'It's murder.'

'No. Each gladiator has a chance and it's up to him to make

the best of it. Now, watch the next event and pay special attention to the *retiarius*. Remember that you could be in his place. That you *will* be in his place. Watch and, for the love of the gods girl, learn. Learn!'

CHAPTER SIXTEEN

It was close to dusk when we left the amphitheatre, and the women were in no condition to travel. They had walked all night, had worked hard the previous day, and the excitement of the display had left them wearied in body and mind. Even so I headed at once towards Rome, keeping them moving until we had covered several miles before settling down for the night.

Camp was made in a hollow well away from the road, a sheltered place close to a running stream in which the women bathed before returning to the fire to eat. I'd bought food from a farm: eggs, bread, cold sausage, olive oil, and some barley together with a pot in which to boil it. Salt and spices provided added flavour, and some thin wine helped to wash it down.

It was dark by the time we had finished, the stars and moon providing a cold luminescence. Waiting until the women had settled, Agonestes and I went to bathe. The water was cold, its sting washing away fatigue as well as dirt, and we rubbed each other down as we stood on the bank.

Dressed Agonestes said, 'Was it worth it, Atilus?'

'We cleared expenses on our bets.'

'I wasn't thinking of that. Did the women learn?'

If they hadn't, they needed to be blind, deaf, and stupid and yet I knew what he meant.

'I'm not sure. Claudia did, I think, and Pholis from her expression. The Nubians regarded it as a holiday, but we can drive the lesson home. Some of the others, perhaps, it's too early to tell.'

'And Verdalia?'

'I don't know. I hope so.'

'I was watching her,' he said. 'Did you know that most of the time her eyes were on you and not on the arena?'

'No.'

'When Claudia grew excited, I noticed Verdalia's eyes. They held hate and anger, not for you but for the woman. Maybe that's the answer, Atilus. Make her jealous and she'd fight like a tiger.'

'Perhaps.'

'I'm certain of it.' His voice held a firm conviction. 'I've seen it happen. Before you came to the school, there was a man who wanted a certain *retiarius*. He was a Thracian but the man he loved preferred another. One day they were matched and the Thracian was superb.'

'And?'

'He died later. As you said, Atilus, in the arena a man has no friends.'

His voice held a note of bitterness and I wondered what had driven home the first lesson any gladiator had to learn. Had he been the *retiarius*? Had he been forced to kill a lover when they faced each other on the sand?

I shivered a little, a chill not born of cold, and thanked the gods that we both were free. In my life I had known few friends, and the thought of having to face Agonestes, of having to kill him or allowing him to kill me, was something unpleasant to entertain.

'Let's get back,' I said. 'And check the guards.'

The three had been carefully chosen, grizzled veterans whose blood was running cold, old campaigners used to going without sleep and who would not be easily tempted by the proximity of women. One crouched before the fire warming his hands. His companions had taken up positions of guard beyond the little camp.

'Villius, you and Nerva get some sleep. We'll stay up with Baebius and call you later.'

'No need,' he grunted. 'A little trip like this is nothing. Why, when I was serving in Judea we went a whole week once without sleep and four days without food.'

That had been years ago when he was young, but I didn't remind him of it. Instead I said, 'Do as I say, Villius. There could be bandits around and I want to keep us all fresh.'

'Judea,' mused Agonestes. 'I've heard talk of that place. A difficult people, yes?'

'They're all mad.' Villius spat into the fire. 'The god they worship sends them that way. The rules and laws they have to live by make normal life impossible. Then they have to contend with their priests and temple dues as well as ordinary taxes. And vicious!' He shook his head. 'Ordinary Jews are bad enough what with their damned airs of superiority, but the Zealots are really something. They refuse to accept the authority of Rome. At night they creep into the camps and cut throats, and the gods help any legionaire they catch on his own. Their women are as bad. I could tell you things you wouldn't believe possible.'

'Try us,' urged Agonestes.

The man hesitated, glancing at the women sprawled all around, but all seemed to be fast asleep.

'They have spiteful ways. Once a patrol was attacked on the way to some village where there was a little trouble. I forget exactly what it was now, probably one of their rabble-rousers telling them not to pay taxes, there was a lot of that. And a preacher of theirs didn't help. He was some agitator who got himself crucified, and his followers claimed he was a god of some kind. Anyway, the lads were attacked and beaten. They were stripped and buried naked in the sand so that only their heads showed. Honey was poured over their faces and it had attracted the ants. By the time we found them the flesh had been eaten to the bone.'

'Were they alive?'

'Those who were had gone out of their minds. We had to kill them.' Villius spat again into the fire. 'Their women did that, and it was common to find a man with his privates cut off and shoved into his mouth so that he choked on his own balls. And they used to stake out men in the sun and cut off their eyelids.

A lousy place and crazy people. I was damned glad to get out of it.'

'Those followers of that god you mentioned,' said Agonestes. 'They're Christians, aren't they?'

'That's what they call themselves.' Villius scowled at painful memory. 'I knew one once. A widow who had a nice little bakery and needed a man to help run it for her. She liked me and I could have done a lot worse. Her face wasn't much but her figure was magnificent, and I could have arranged with the centurion to have been put on civil-posting. That's done a lot out there,' he explained. 'And more in Greece. When things are quiet or when the procurator wants to ease tension, he'll give permission for some legionaires to be semi-released to work at civilian occupations. We'd be on call, naturally, and have to tend our arms, but mainly we work and sleep away from camp. It's got advantages both ways, of course; a man in such a position can pick up a lot of useful information.'

'And?'

'She was a Christian,' he said bitterly. 'I didn't mind that, Rome allows everyone to worship in their own fashion as long as they acknowledge Caesar, and I was even willing to forego the usual household lares, but she wasn't satisfied with that. She wanted to convert me. I ask you! Me, a soldier, having to promise to turn the other cheek if anyone hit me! Naturally I couldn't agree, so that was the end of it. A pity,' he mourned. 'A nice business and a body men dream about when on watch at night. Well, that's life.'

'You and Nerva get some sleep now,' I insisted. 'We'll keep watch.'

Muttering, he went to call the other, the two of them settling down beneath the shadow of a bush, Villius to dream, perhaps, of his lost opportunity.

Rising from where I had squatted, I moved around the fire, counting the women. All were present, some snoring, a few twitching restlessly. Verdalia lay with one arm across her eyes, her chest rising and falling with a steady regularity.

The remaining guard turned as I approached him, steel glimmering naked in his hand.

'All right, Baebius, it's us.'

He nodded at Agonestes and then looked hard at me.

'I'm not trying to catch you out,' I said. 'Just checking. Heard anything?'

'Nothing to worry about.' His sword made a thin, rasping sound as he returned it to its scabbard. 'A couple of owls and a fox barking. We're safe enough here.'

He was probably right, though men could hoot like owls, and the bark of a fox made a good signal. In any case I was too tense to remain idle and Agonestes guessed the reason.

'You're thinking of Verdalia,' he accused as we made a circuit of the camp. 'Atilus, she'll live or die by her own decision. You can't fight for her and you can't stop her from having to fight.'

'Maybe I can.'

'No, Atilus,' he said gently. 'We've been over that. She is an imperial slave. You can't buy her and set her free. You can't help her to escape. If she is unsuited to the arena, Nero will dispose of her, not you. Man,' he snapped as I shook my head, 'think it out. Do you think those other women won't talk? That some of the guards haven't already been bribed. If you try to make a fool of the Emperor, I shudder to think of what will happen to you. Do you want to join the *andabatae*? To fight blind, slashing at air, waiting to feel the bite of a sword, knowing that death is inevitable? Do you want to be crucified? Get some sense, Atilus! What is one woman the more or less to you?'

Nothing, and yet Verdalia was something special, as he knew, and while appreciating his advice I couldn't take it. Somehow there had to be a way. Heraculis could juggle the books and falsify the entries, but even as I considered it I knew it to be hopeless. The certificates of transfer were on local record. People would talk and, as an imperial agent, I was bound by the laws of Rome.

To defy the Emperor was to invite a horrible death.

'Be hard,' urged Agonestes. 'Atilus, be hard!'

A voice which whispered to me from the darkness as years ago in my dreams, another voice had urged me to be strong. The voice of my mother.

'Live, Atilus' she had said. 'Live!'

Back at the fire nothing seemed to have changed and yet, immediately, I knew that something was wrong. Quickly I counted the women, finding one missing, knowing who it was even before I looked.

'Verdalia!' Agonestes sucked in his breath. 'Maybe she's gone to ease herself.'

A hope which died as I examined the bank of the stream. Returning I said, 'Wait here.'

'Atilus let—'

'Wait!'

I was running before he could answer, bending low so as to see the skyline. She could have been gone only minutes, waiting until Baebius had moved away, taking advantage of my absence to plunge into the night. A woman, alone, where would she hide? The bushes were scanty and it was natural that I should have searched the banks of the stream. The terrain was unfamiliar and would slow her progress. Any hiding place she might find would shield her only until the day and, it was instinctive for a runaway to put as much distance behind him as possible.

Halting, crouched, I listened.

From somewhere an owl hooted. Closer, a rustle signalled the passage of some nocturnal beast. Ahead and to my right a branch snapped with a thin, betraying sound. I ran towards it and the road beyond. On the paved way she could make better time, overlooking in her haste the dangers it held. Road patrols would question a lone woman wearing the tunic of a slave, and others she might meet would hold her in hope of a reward.

Again came the sound of something large and heavy breaking through the bushes and, this time, I caught a glimpse of something occluding the stars. Reaching the road, I dropped so as to remain hidden, waiting until a shape appeared in the soft illumination. A woman with hair silvered to match the strained pallor of her face.

She gasped as I rose up beside her.

'Verdalia, why be such a fool?'

'You!' For a moment it seemed that she would reach towards me and then she said, bitterly, 'Is that what you call it?'

'How far do you think you will get? To the place we have just left? And then what? You have no money, no friends. Who is going to feed you, hide you, lie on your behalf?'

'I can work.'

'Where? As what? Not even a brothel keeper would take in a runaway slave.' I reached out and took her wrist. 'Let's get back.'

'To what? The arena? Do you want to see me slaughtered like those others? Watch, you said. Watch and learn. Well, I've learned. Not you, not anyone will ever master me!'

She was magnificent in her rage, an anger which triggered my own so that I felt the blood pound in my ears and the breath clog in my lungs.

'You stupid bitch! Can't you understand? I don't want to see you hurt. By all the gods, I—'

For answer she tried to kick me in the groin.

Instinct saved me, that and the gleam of her naked foot as it rose. A foot which slammed on my thigh as I twisted, to duck to avoid her hands reaching for my eyes, to see stars as her elbow jarred against the side of my head.

And then, at once, we were fighting.

It was raw, primeval combat, divorced from the skilled interplay of swords, the calculated movements of shield and foot. Like a wild animal she tried to rend and tear and, like a wild animal, I fought back. Not to hurt her, not to cripple or maim, but to hold, to grip, to master.

The road was built up from the ground. We fell from it, rolling, to part and meet again, starlight gleaming from her eyes and bared teeth, moonlight shimmering from her hair.

Her tunic ripped beneath my hand, breasts showing clear, swelling mounds tipped with circles black in the light, the nipples full and prominent. Her hands clawed at my loins, seeking to rip, to twist and tear. I pushed her away and the remains of the tunic fell to leave her completely naked.

'Verdalia!'

She was distorted, her eyes wild with a passion I had seen before on the faces of women who watched blood and pain on the sand. Like a fury she rushed at me and, with equal fury I grabbed at her, consumed now with a sudden onset of lust which swelled my manhood with a demanding tumescence. A passion which was returned as together we fell, her face lifted to the stars, her legs rising to lock about my waist, her arms around my neck, her lips seeking and pressing hard against my own while the fluids of her desire laved the flesh which I thrust between her thighs.

A woman conquered.

A woman changed.

'Atilus, did you know how I felt? I wanted, by the gods how I wanted you to take me, and yet something inside wouldn't let me yield.'

The ice which had contained her fury, had distorted it, blinding her to the basic fact of life. Existence is paramount—dead you can do nothing.

'I love you,' I said. 'Verdalia, I love you.'

'And I you, Atilus.' Her hand rose to touch my hair. Beneath us the grass was cool against our skins as, both naked now, we lay on the spot which had witnessed our passion. 'I think that I loved you from the first, but how could I love a Roman?'

'I'm not a Roman.'

'I know. And I know now that, all along, you have tried to be kind. Perhaps too kind; women are quick to take advantage of what they consider to be weakness. You are strong, Atilus, and you must show them that. Only the strong are respected.'

'Is that why I had to fight you?'

'Perhaps.' Her smile was enigmatic. 'Do you think I can fight?'

'Like a wildcat—when you are willing.'

'And I will be willing. Now that I have something to live for, I will show these Romans how a woman of my race can do battle.' She turned to look at me, her eyes lambent in the silvery glow from the skies. 'You have given me life, Atilus. For the first time since the Romans came to my village, I have a reason to survive.'

I thought of Agonestes who, despite his indifference to women, had been so right in his judgement. He would be waiting for our return and I said so.

'He can wait,' she whispered. 'Darling, he can wait.'

Her arms closed around me, holding me a prisoner in a delightful cage from which I never wanted to escape.

CHAPTER SEVENTEEN

'Helvidius, are you sure?' I looked at Agonestes as he sat perched on the edge of the table in the office of the school. He wore his best finery, his hair a mass of neat curls, the air scented with his perfume. His eyes were puffed a little and his face lax with fatigue and dissipation. Long days and longer nights had worn him down, finally, he had gained the information. 'Grypus Helvidius?'

'The same.'

'There's no mistake?'

'None. Cadius was clear on the point. I would have tried to get the information earlier, but I had to be careful. First our relationship had to be firmly established.' Agonestes brushed a fleck of lint from his tunic. It was of silk ornamented with pearls, a gift from the young patrician who was now his lover. 'An odd young man,' he mused. 'One with an active imagination yet unexpected depths of delicacy. And he is insatiable.'

For now, but passion quickly aroused could as quickly die, as he knew too well.

'Helvidius,' I said. 'I might have guessed it.'

'You know him?'

'We've met.'

It had been years ago now, when first I had left Rome to make my way in provincial arenas. Young, inexperienced in the ways of roving *lanistae*, I had joined his *familia* and had almost died as a result. Hard, brutal, the man had thoughts only for himself. He had matched me with a *myrmillo* and hinted that the man was old, needed to be nursed and that, if I fell, my life was assured. Almost I had believed him, and only an instinct for danger had allowed me to avoid the trap. Bets had been arranged and the *myrmillo*, though old, was cunning. Only the gods had saved me and a scar on my right thigh still ached when it rained.

'Apparently he ran into some trouble down in Tarentum,' said Agonestes. 'He went too far and lost most of his *familia* aside from a few broken slaves whose owners didn't know the man's reputation or didn't care. Then he tried a novelty, five pairs of women fighting as *myrmillones*. I don't know if Nero knew of it when he gave you your assignment, but he certainly does now. Cadius or someone must have mentioned it and pointed out that two different groups of gladiators would provide better fun than one. Anyway, money and orders were sent and now Helvidius is an imperial agent.'

'Like me,' I said bitterly.

'Not like you,' corrected Agonestes. 'The man is totally devoid of all feeling. Cadius didn't go into detail, but we can guess how he's training his women.'

With fire and whips and red-hot irons. With floggings and crucifixions, maiming and blinding, bodies tormented to provide sickening examples. His fighters would be animals, terrified to lose, creatures conditioned and taught by brutality and pain.

'A syndicate has been formed to handle the betting,' said Agomestes. 'That's why Cadius was snooping around. He keeps asking me questions and he wants to pay another visit.' Again he touched his tunic. 'This was a bribe. I asked for another—a thousand gold pieces to be wagered on my behalf. On Helvidius, of course.'

So it was to be a matter, not of individual fighters but of the men who had trained them. My women against those of Helvidius. My reputation against his.

'The odds?'

'Against you three to one.' Agonestes was bland. 'With luck we can stretch them to four or even five. A chance to make a killing, Atilus, if we handle it right.'

And he knew how to do it. The suggested bribe coupled with false information and what Cadius himself had seen would make the syndicate confident of picking up an easy fortune. Weeks ago that would have been inevitable, but things had changed.

The proof lay in the practice ground. The women, now hard at their training, had gained a new determination. A resolve to win induced by what they had seen, maintained and enhanced by Verdalia who had added her strength to my own.

Strength of a different kind. For her mercy was a word inapplicable to enemies, and the one who faced her on the sand was an enemy. A woman, she knew of the tricks and drives of her own sex and, as a woman, she had none of my reluctance to be savagely harsh.

Agonestes grunted his satisfaction as he saw her weave over the ground, net and trident busy, the sunlight gleaming from her oiled flesh. She fought now as she would fight in the arena, naked but for her belt and frontal apron, the armour on her shoulder, the fillet which held back the golden mane of her hair.

'Beautiful,' murmured Agonestes. 'Those breasts and buttocks—she will send the crowd wild.'

The *secutar* facing her was a little slow. Trying to dodge she was muffled in the net, falling as it jerked.

'You stupid cow!' Reversing the trident Verdalia rammed the butt into the woman's stomach. 'You're dead, do you hear? Dead!' Again the punishing blow of the shaft emphasised the lesson. 'Now get up and try again.'

'No!' Stepping forward I gestured the winded woman to one side. 'Take on another.'

'Why?' Verdalia was harsh. 'She has to learn.'

'And so do you. What do you hope to gain from an opponent who is beaten before she starts?' Turning I saw Pholis and waved for her to take position. 'A vial of perfume to the one who wins. Go!'

Gifts to the victor, scorn and bruises to those who failed, a combination appealing to pride and vanity and which seemed to work.

'She's improved,' said Agonestes as he watched the encounter. 'Pholis isn't bad but Verdalia is good. You must have been giving her extra training.'

Long hours during which I had pressed her hard, teaching her speed, the way to anticipate, the way to dodge. Things I should have taught as well to the others, but there had been no time and none as special to me as she was.

That night, when she came to me in my chamber, I said, 'You were slow and a little careless. You're getting overconfident and that's a fault which could kill you.'

'Preaching, darling?'

'Trying to keep you alive.'

She smiled and came closer towards me. The perfume she had won threw an odorous cloud over her body and hair, and it filled my nostrils with the essence of flowers.

'You worry too much, Atilus,' she murmured. 'I can beat any other woman here and you know it. I could even beat you.'

A challenge—always she had to challenge. Before she would yield she had to be mastered, a secret desire to be ravished, perhaps, or the need to be reassured that the man who used her was stronger than herself. A trait both stimulating and wearisome, yet still I loved her, still the magic of her body possessed me.

Two swords lay on the bed, practice weapons, blunt but capable of breaking bones and bruising flesh.

'Learn,' I said, and threw her one.

Germans used the broadsword, their women often fighting at their side, so she was no stranger to the weapon. Lifting, she ran at me, steel clashing as I easily parried the cut, the flat of my own blade stinging her thigh. Again she attacked, again to meet the barrier of my sword. Snarling, consumed with fury now, she hurled herself at me. Smiling I backed, parried, turned aside her blade, sent my own to sting her flesh.

'Do you still think you can beat me?'

"With this, no.' She lowered the sword, panting. 'But with a net and trident—'

'Against me you wouldn't have a chance.' I was deliberately contemptuous. 'I would know what you were going to do before you did it. I would cut you, your breasts, your buttocks, your thighs. You let anger control you instead of remaining cool.'

'You told me that anger can be useful.'

'Only while you control it. It sharpens the concentration and gives added strength. But it isn't enough simply to hate. Rage doesn't give skill and it won't frighten an experienced fighter. Now, try again. Thrust, don't cut, and don't waste energy on wild movements. Come on!' I snapped as she hesitated. 'Your body is the prize.'

A prize I won as I had known I would. Won and used, later to lie watching the play of lamplight on the ceiling.

'Atilus.' Her hand ran up my naked chest, the fingers walking as if they had been the legs of an insect. 'Atilus, do you love me?'

'Yes, too much.'

'Can a man love a woman too much?'

'When she is wilful, strange, difficult to understand, and hard to live with, yes.'

'Am I those things?' Rearing she looked down at me, her eyes shadowed by the cascade of her hair. 'Am I?'

'I've known others easier to get along with.'

'Patricians,' she said contemptuously. 'Spoiled and degenerate bitches who want slaves for lovers, not men. Can they give you what I can?'

'More,' I said, teasing her. 'Gold and silk and valuable presents. They have influence and can advance a man's career. Help him to gain the favour of the Emperor and obtain an official sinecure.'

'And the rest?'

Still teasing I said, 'You know the saying: all cats are grey at night.'

'Don't you dare say that!' The flat of her hand stung my cheek. 'Don't you dare to tell me that, in the dark, all women are the same. If I was blind and had a thousand men, I would know you at once. Atilus, please, tell me that I am special.'

'You are special.'

'Do you mean it?'

'I mean it.' My arms closed around her. 'Verdalia, my darling, you are the loveliest women I have ever known.'

Smiling at the flattery, she ran her hand again over my chest.

'One day, Atilus, you must tell me all about your misty Britain. Did you live in a fine, big house with plenty of cattle and servants?'

'No. We lived in mud and wattle and my mother and I did all the work.'

'But your father was a warrior, surely?'

'He was a trader from Gaul. He vanished before the Romans invaded.' I tried to remember how he had looked, but there were too many years in between. 'I think he must have been killed, perhaps murdered. In any case I never saw him again.'

'And your mother is dead.' In the shadow of her hair her face was serious. 'Agonestes told me about it. He likes you, Atilus. If I were a man I think he would be jealous of me. Do you like him?'

'He is a friend.' To change the subject I said, 'Tell me about your home.'

'In Germany?' She shrugged. 'Our village was set deep in the forests and the men used to hunt and trade with men from the northern coasts. Our tribe is a strong one, which is probably why the Romans attacked. We refused to pay them tribute and so they wanted revenge.' Her voice hardened. "Need I tell you of the habits of Rome?'

The burning, pillaging, and killing as the legions crushed all opposition. The hammer of the state spreading domination, taking captives, making orphans. I was here because of them, and I could imagine the things which must have happened to her. The violation of her body, the rape, the robbing of her virginity.

'They mastered me,' she whispered. 'But I was fortunate.' And then, with a sudden change of tone, she said, 'You would like my home, Atilus, and my people would like you. They respect a warrior. They would give you furs and amber, iron and land. We would have a big house and lots of children.'

'Under Roman rule?'

'They will be gone now. Rome will never conquer Germany. Do you like children?'

'Yes.'

'Good. Atilus, what shall we call our son?'

'Our son?'

'Your seed is growing in my belly,' she said calmly. 'It will be a boy, I am sure of it. A warrior. A man just like his father who planted him in my womb.'

Sitting upright on the bed I lifted the hair from her face and looked into her eyes. 'You're pregnant?'

'I missed a turn of the moon.' She smiled at my expression. 'Don't look so surprised, Atilus. What did you expect? Surely you know how babies are made?'

'Are you sure?'

'Of course.' Her eyes grew hard as she stared at me. 'What's the matter? Don't you want it?'

The child, yes, but not the situation. She was a slave, a gladiator, soon to fight in the area. Pregnant, she would be at a disadvantage and, the longer she waited the worse it would be.

And the sword which sent her to the sand would kill not one, but two.

'Atilus?'

'I was thinking,' I lied. 'Of a name. Verdalia, you have given me the world!'

The answer she wanted, and the lie was worth the happiness which illuminated her face. Holding her, I looked at the window, the night outside. Tomorrow I would think about it. She could be mistaken or lying and, even if she wasn't, something could be arranged. Tomorrow I would see about it. But the next day I was summoned to the presence of Nero.

CHAPTER EIGHTEEN

He sat in a courtyard cooled by tingling fountains, resting on a couch and dressed all in purple and gold. A dish of succulent dainties stood on a table beside him and slaves wafted scented breezes over his head and shoulders with wide fans of ostrich feathers which they waved over containers of perfume. Poppaea sat at his side, resplendent in a stola of silk encrusted with gems, and I recognised others: Seneca, Petronius, Cadius Publius, who nodded me a greeting, Burrus, the Praetorian Prefect, who studiously ignored me. Others, strangers, stood in casual attitudes, sycophants all, most wanting some personal advantage.

As I advanced to fall on one knee before him, Nero beamed and extended his hand.

'My dear, Atilus, you have arrived in splendid time. I am just about to sing.'

Rising, he gargled with liquid from a crystal flask, spitting it out into a bowl held by an attendant slave. Picking up a lyre, he struck a chord and, without preamble, burst into song.

It was something to do with unrequited love, the perfidy of women, and the nobility of self-sacrifice, and I guessed that he had composed it himself. His voice was better than the song, but neither merited the storm of praise which followed when he lowered the lyre. Praise in which I joined, my voice loud enough to be heard even if my flattery was more restrained than the rest.

'You are all too kind,' said Nero, touching his eyes with a scrap of silk. 'Well you know how much an artist needs an appreciation of his work, and yet to utter empty compliments would not be kind. Burrus, what did you think? Be honest now.'

The man was a grizzled veteran, scarred from old campaigns, a dedicated servant of Rome and the Emperor. Now, gruffly, he said, 'I'm only a simple soldier and haven't the words to express myself, but to me you sang better than anyone I've ever heard.'

'An honest, simple compliment from an honest, simple man,' said Petronius, and I guessed that he and Burrus were friends. 'Who could ask for more? Only those who seek to mask their true thoughts with words utter fullsome phrases when an expression of fact will suffice.'

'Atilus?'

'I am a man of the arena,' I said. 'To me the ring of blades and the roar of the crowd applauding my victory are sweet music. Yet what I have heard here today has diminished my pleasure in all other artists.'

Others followed with their comments and, in the noise, I didn't hear the arrival of another guest. Racilia Rubinia, her face pale beneath the crown of her auburn hair, paid her respects to the Emperor together with an apology for her tardiness.

'My sedan was blocked by the crowd, Nero. They are thick at the foot of Palatine.'

'Always the crowd!' His face darkened, and a slave ran forward with a vial at which he sniffed. 'What is it this time? More riots over the shortage of bread? The price of grain and oil? Burras, why can't you rid me of this trouble? What are the Praetorians doing to allow it?'

'My men have their orders, Caesar. They will guard you with their lives.'

'Isn't that what they are paid for?' Nero was cold. 'Have them disperse the crowd immediately.'

Saluting, Burras went to obey and Nero sat, his face shrouded in gloom. He was, I guessed, thinking of a recent incident when his statue had been found with a sack over the head. The inference was plain: according to Roman law a patricide or a matricide was condemned to be tied in a sack together with a snake, a cockerel, and a cat, and flung to drown in the Tiber. The act had been a public implication that Nero had killed his mother.

The truth, but he couldn't be expected to like it, and neither did others, but for different reasons. I had noticed the crowds myself when obeying Nero's summons. Small groups of men had gathered at the street corners, larger factions running down the avenues, and the Roman mob, notoriously volatile, could turn in a moment to an orgy of rioting.

The presence of Racilia disturbed me. We had not met since the night at the school when we had reached an agreement, and from her expression I knew that she was uneasy.

'You are distraught, Nero,' said Petronius. 'And we all understand the strain you are under and the demands made by your art. Yet you have guests and—'

'It would be in bad taste to ignore them. My arbiter, what would I do without you?' Nero, his gloom forgotten, stretched out his hands towards us. 'Racilia, Atilus, come to me. You two know each other, I believe?'

I spoke quickly before she could deny it.

'Yes, Nero, we've met.'

'Dare I ask when and where?' His tone was mild but I knew him too well to be deluded. Spies would have kept him informed and others, eager for favour, would have been quick to cast suspicion. He relaxed as I explained that, together, we had travelled from Aricia. 'And later?' The wave of his hand dismissed the need for me to answer. 'Perhaps it would not be well to go into that, eh? A lovely woman married to an old man. I try hard to maintain a high moral standard as everyone is aware, but youth must have its fling. But no matter. Racilia, I want your advice on a certain subject, but before we discuss it, there is something else. Atilus, how are you progressing with your female gladiators?'

Conscious of Cadius and his listening ears I said, 'Badly, I'm afraid. There has been no time to produce good fighters. They will do their best, but it will be poor.'

'Slow? Clumsy?'

'Both,' I admitted. 'Another year and—'

'That is impossible!'

Bowing I said, 'I am yours to command, my Emperor. The women will fight whenever you so decide.'

'The people are restless,' he said. 'They need something to take their minds off imagined grievances. I shall give a display of gladiators, and your women can fight then. I hope that we shall not be disappointed, Atilus.'

'They are evenly matched,' I said. 'Against skilled fighters, of course, they would be useless, but their novelty may appeal to the crowd. In a few months I should have them ready.'

'Not months, Atilus, days.' Nero held out his hand and a slave placed the smelling bottle in his palm. 'The people must be calmed. You agree, Gaius?'

Petronius shrugged. 'Always they need to be calmed, Nero, but your music would be far more effective.'

'How can I deny it.' Nero rolled his eyes upwards. 'The gods alone know how hard I have tried. Plays written by myself in which I have taken a personal interest. Songs together with dances, and still they are not satisfied. A man can only do so much. Before they can appreciate my art, their barbaric appetites must be fed. Very well, if blood they want, then blood they will have. In three days' time, Atilus, your women must be ready.'

Again I bowed. The words had been a dismissal, but still I lingered.

'With respect, my Emperor, a suggestion. One which I am sure will appeal to your sense of fairness. The women are slaves. If I could tell them that they will be freed if they should win...?'

Seneca rasped, 'You go too far! Slaves should not be bribed with promises. It is their duty to obey.'

'They are women,' said Racilia. She was more relaxed now, grateful to me for having spoken. 'A woman needs an incentive if she is to put out her best.'

'Gaius?'

'As they will probably be laughed from the amphitheatre,

Nero, does it matter? Already they have been ruined as obedient slaves. I agree with Atilus, give them a spur and, like a horse, they will work all the harder.' He added, casually, 'From what I understand, few if any will be left alive.'

A hint that he knew of what was going on, and could even be a member of the wagering syndicate. Then I caught his eyes and knew better. Wise, cynical, with all the money he could possibly need, he would not be concerned with such trivia.

Seneca decided the issue. Again his voice rasped over the tinkling of the fountains.

'You cannot do it, Nero. Who knows where such an example may lead? Slaves are to be ruled and they must obey. Do you promise a dog a reward when you whistle him to heel? Let the women fight, but promise them nothing. Do not undermine the authority of Rome.'

How often in the past must Nero have heard that thin, spiteful voice commanding him to obey? Now he heard it again, but he was no longer dependent on others. Deliberately he ignored his old tutor.

'Gaius, you are right, what does it matter? Atilus, I have decided. The women will be freed if they win.'

Bowing, I gave him my thanks and then wandered around the courtyard. Later the place would be full of guests invited to one of Nero's banquets at which he would entertain, but now the palace was almost empty.

'Atilus!' Racilia came towards me, her talk with Nero completed, and she guessed that I had been waiting for her. Lowering her voice, she said, 'I was about to deny that we'd met. Why did you say otherwise?'

We stood before a statue imported from Greece. Looking at the bright colours I said, equally quietly, 'Never lie when the truth will serve. We met—and I said nothing of how we parted. If he knows, he will put it down to a lover's quarrel.'

'He asked about you,' she said. 'That night at the school. Can no one be trusted?'

'No one. Did you follow my advice?'

'I would rather have eaten dirt, but, yes, I did. Julius is being recalled to Rome. A favour Nero was pleased to grant, but at a price.' She shook her head at my expression. 'Not that, Atilus. Nero wants me to bear witness against Octavia. She is virtuous, as everyone knows, but he wants to divorce her in order to marry Poppaea. I am to lie so that he may gain his own ends. Well, that lies in the future, but what hope has Rome when such a monster rules?'

'Be careful! Walls have ears!'

'He's mad,' she said flatly. 'He giggled when he told me what I must do. The ruin of a decent woman, and he regards it as a joke.' Her breasts lifted as she drew in her breath. 'The gods will surely take revenge on his vile ways.'

'Then leave it to the gods,' I said curtly. 'Plotters make uneasy companions.'

'Yes,' she admitted. 'But a word, Atilus, I know something which could be important to you.'

I sensed what was coming, but did not make the mistake of anticipating it. Even when she told me, my face reflected nothing but surprise.

'Grypus Helvidius?'

'A hard, brutal man, Atilus. His women are to fight yours. A jest of Nero's. Cadius told me about it and urged me to lay wagers against you.'

'And the women?'

'Are in Rome. They arrived this morning and are housed in a villa belonging to Aurelius Licinius.'

So he too was involved in the syndicate, even though absent. A bad sign; with money to burn, slaves could be bribed and officials suborned, convenient accidents made to happen if for any reason they suspected they might lose. It was time for me to take precautions.

Thoughtfully I looked at Racilia. She had reason to trust me—could I her? There had been no need for her to have told me what she had, and she could have no inkling that the news was stale. And she had the ear of the Emperor. Nero, capricious and wilful, would relish a joke, and his favour would provide a defence if one was needed.

'Racilia, I need your help.' I smiled at her expression. 'Nothing serious. Just a loan of five thousand pieces of gold. I will repay it within a month. For security you have myself.'

For a moment she hesitated, then said, 'Agreed. You pay within a month or you bind yourself to me for a year under contract to fight as and when I direct. All prizes and fees to be mine.'

A hard bargain, but in many ways she was a hard woman.

'And one thing more, Racilia. A hint to be given to Nero, but to no one else. Have I your word?' I saw her frown as if at an implied threat and added, quickly, 'It could help you and can do you no harm. Just, when you are alone and none can overhear, mention that you are convinced I will win.'

'Will you?' Her eyes met mine and then, slowly, she nodded. 'Cadius is young and a fool. He is too impressed by Helvidius and he doesn't know you as I do. Should you win, Nero will thank me and, Atilus, I shall thank you.'

From the palace I went directly to the Great School where Gallus Caecina greeted me with a smile and offered me wine.

As we drank he said, 'You're looking well, Atilus, but a little drawn about the eyes. It must be all those women. Fight all day and ride all night, eh? That's no life for a gladiator. If you aren't careful, you'll be getting soft.'

'I'm fit enough.'

'Are you?' His glance was shrewd. 'Teaching *tiros* is no way to maintain your edge. Like to prove that I'm wrong? I've a *retiarius* from Spain who will be a first-class fighter if he manages to survive. A little rough, but he can be smoothed and he has the right spirit. How about a practice bout? I've a couple of gold pieces to ride on him if you want to bet.'

'I've five hundred—they could be yours.'

'How?'

His face darkened as I told him. Slamming down his goblet he said, 'Atilus, you're mad! Women in the school? It's unthinkable!'

'Only until the *munera*,' I urged. 'That's three days from now.'

'I know. Short notice, but Nero has to quiet the public, and now he wants to include women gladiators.' Gallus shook his head; a man disgusted with the indecent proposal. 'Once a good, clean fight was enough,' he said bitterly. 'Trained pairs fighting to kill and die, and teaching Romans how to be brave. Now everything has to be a novelty: exotic animals, girls raped by apes and donkeys, men torn apart by horses. Where's the skill in that?'

No skill, only blood and pain, but that is what the public wanted and, what a Roman crowd demanded, they got.

'Five hundred pieces of gold, Gallus,' I said. 'Yours for the use of a few rooms to house my women until the display.'

'No.'

'They are gladiators ordered by the Emperor. As imperial slaves, they have the right to be here.'

'Not as far as I'm concerned.'

'The law—'

'Be damned to the law! They have no right here and you know it. There's no precedent. Take the matter to the magistrates if you want, but you'll be wasting your time.' Snorting, he poured us more wine and, in a calmer tone said, 'Now drink up and be sensible. When you asked me to help you before, I could do it. One man among so many, what difference did it make? But a bunch of women, stripping, training—how can a thing like that be kept quiet?'

It couldn't and I knew it, but by asking too much at first, he would be more inclined to grant me what I really wanted.

'A dozen men,' I said. 'To act as sparring partners and to keep watch over the women.'

'Instructors?' Frowning he shook his head. 'I can't spare them, Atilus, and even if I could they wouldn't be willing.'

'Not instructors.' It was too late for that and their advice would conflict with my own. 'Just men to fight in practice and to stand guard. Men I can trust.'

He looked at me from beneath his eyebrows and I guessed that he must have heard rumours. Certainly he recognised the dangers and, as I explained the position, he nodded.

'Helvidius is a bad one and I can guess your concern. A few broken bones, something in their wine or food, I'd put nothing past him. You'll have to watch out for yourself too, Atilus. Stay away from dark alleys.'

'I intend to. And the men?'

'I'll find you some. A score, not a dozen. They'll be at your place before dark, and they won't cost you five hundred pieces.'

'You'll take it, Gallus. For the men, your trouble and,' I added meaningfully, 'for any other help you can give.'

CHAPTER NINETEEN

The day of the *munera* broke with mist and a thin veil of cloud whitening the sky. A good sign; later it would burn away, but now it softened the fury of the sun and gave a brisk crispness to the air. I had not permitted the women to participate in the customary feast held in the arena the previous night. As contenders they had the right to attend, but they were hysterical gatherings with degenerates of both sexes bringing gifts of food, wine, and tawdry ornaments; bribes which they offered the gladiators as they touched and fondled them and offered the use of their bodies for sexual release. Instead, I had made them retire early, standing guard over them as if they had been rare and precious jewels instead of women, many of whom would never see another night.

Not even Verdalia could tempt me.

'Atilus,' she protested, 'why not? What harm could it do?'

'It could tire you, slow you down, take the edge off your concentration. Later, after you've won, we can make love, but not now.'

'And if I should die?'

'Then you die!' I was harsh. 'But I'll have nothing to reproach myself with. Now get to bed and get some sleep.'

It had been a long night, but now it was over. The women had risen two hours before dawn, eaten a light meal, bathed, performed a few limbering up exercises, and were now safe in the preparation room of the arena.

Gallus had earned his money. The room was the best available, discreet officials standing around and preventing anyone getting too close. Twice they had rejected gifts of wine from unknown well-wishers—wine which could have held added ingredients. The third time a slave brought an amphora I took it, thanked him, waited until he had gone, then bribed an official to take it to where Helvidius kept his women.

The ceremonial procession gave me the chance to study them, and they were what I'd expected; hard, mannish creatures, their bodies thick with welts and oozing sores from recent burns. A typical product of the man himself.

Grypus Helvidius was broad, stocky, his face ridged with seams and scars. Almost totally bald, his scalp bore mottled patches, the fringe of hair scented and curled, hanging low over his ears. His teeth were rotting and his breath stank. An ex-gladiator. A *myrmillo* who had turned *lanista*, sending others to fight and using them as a farmer used cattle.

'Atilus!' His smile held no humour as, after the procession, we faced each other in the shadows beyond the Gate of Life. 'So we meet again.'

'So it would seem.'

'A joke,' he said. 'Trust the Emperor to have his fun. Is it true that you've pledged yourself on the outcome?'

In Rome gossip travelled quickly.

'A pity,' he said as I made no answer. 'But afterwards, maybe, we can get together. I can always use a good fighter. Marius, let's get to work!'

Marius, his assistant, was a dour man built like a *pugile*, younger than Helvidius, but bearing the same stamp of savage brutality. Now he used his whip with careless abandon as he ushered his women back to their room.

To my own I said, 'Well, you've seen them. They are the women you have to fight. Now remember what I told you. Don't lose your heads. Don't look at the crowd. Don't try to be clever. And, above all, don't hope for mercy. You won't get it. You either kill or be killed. You fight for life and freedom. Now get ready.'

Together with Agonestes, I checked every item of equipment,

the shields, the protective armour, the fit of helmets and belts. Tugging at Verdalia's, I tightened it a little. Pholis grunted as I pulled at her greave.

'It'll do as it is.'

'It's loose. Out there you're going to sweat, and the straps may slip. Now, all of you, make sacrifice to the gods.'

An empty precaution, perhaps, but I was leaving nothing to chance. As the smoke rose before the grimed images, the trumpets sounded, officials bawling for us to get ready. As the deep, solemn notes echoed again we ran through the Gate of Life and out onto the sand.

Helena was the first to die.

She was the leggy Greek *retiarius* and she was dragged from the arena, her hair hanging loose, one breast almost severed, her intestines bulging from the slash across her belly.

The woman who had killed her was a Thracian, sacrificing protection for greater mobility. Blood ran from one cheek where Helena had caught her with her trident, but she had aimed too low and missed the eyes. A mistake which had cost her her life.

'The eyes!' Agonestes's voice rose above the lash of his whip. 'Aim for the eyes!'

Together he and I ran from one of our fighters to the other, urging, directing, using our whips to keep them at it.

Helvidius and Marius were doing the same, but their blows were more vicious, flesh and blood showing where their leaded thongs had struck.

Another went down, one of my Nubians shrieking with fury as she slammed the trident into the fallen woman's guts. A fault, she should have waited for the verdict of the crowd, for Nero's signal from where he watched, lounging in his ornate chair on the podium.

But neither he nor the crowd seemed to care. Their voices rose in a yelling thunder.

'Atilus! Atilus! Atilus!'

My name, shouted as was that of Helvidius, each of us the centre of attention. A result of an addition by Julius Asprenas, the Master of Games. Each of the women wore a coloured plume in helmet or hair; red for me and blue for Helvidius. Another novelty: gladiators did not fight as members of a team but as individuals. It was proof of the disdain in which Asprenas held them that they were classed as members of a faction, wearing colours as did the teams in a chariot race.

'Helvidius! Get in there!'

Yet another of my women had fallen, a *secutor*, throwing aside her shield and lifting her hand for mercy. A plea denied as the crowd jeered and Nero negligently turned down his thumb.

He was enjoying himself, his face creased in a smile, one hand caressing Poppaea's thigh as she sat close at his side. As the *retiarius* lifted her trident and stabbed at the shrieking woman's eyes, I saw his tongue protrude like a wet serpent from his mouth, the tip caressing his lower lip.

'Keep at it!' The woman before me was faltering. I sent my whip cracking against her naked flesh. 'Watch the net! In! Use the sword! Use it!'

When the trumpets next sounded, five of my women were dead.

Five of mine as against three belonging to Helvidius, and the crowd left no doubt as to whom they considered would be the final victor.

'Helvidius! Helvidius! Helvidius!'

The roar followed me as I passed through the Gate of Life.

Grinning, Helvidius offered to buy me wine.

'Don't take it too badly, Atilus. We all have to learn. Your trouble is that you were too gentle with them. A few touches of the hot irons can work wonders. Come and have a drink.'

'No.'

'We've time until the next bout. Some Falernian, eh? The best.' His grin grew wider as he looked at my face, seeing what I wanted him to see. 'Don't look so distressed. So you lose—but life goes on.'

For me, perhaps, but not for some of the others. And even those who had walked victorious from the arena would carry scars for the rest of their lives. In the infirmary I watched as a physician called for searing irons. Beneath the hands of attendant slaves, Lavinia writhed and sweated in her pain. A *retiarius*, she had won, but a sword had opened her shoulder to the bone.

'Steady!' I gripped her hand. 'It's over now. You're free.'

'Atilus! I—by the gods, the pain!'

'Opium!' I snapped to the attendants. 'Give her opium!'

'It's been administered, Atilus.' The physician gestured for me to stand aside. 'Now hold her steady. Hold her!'

Smoke rose as he applied the iron, cauterising the wound, sealing it against further loss of blood. With the smoke came the stench of burning meat. On the couch Lavinia reared, eyes wild, mouth open to display her teeth and tongue, the rasp of her scream an agonised shriek.

Then, as she sagged mercifully unconscious, the physician grunted and shook his head.

'Women! What can you expect? They have no pride. Any normal gladiator wouldn't have uttered a sound.'

'Will she be all right?'

'For a while she'll be stiff and always she'll be scarred, but there's nothing to worry about.' The physician examined the wound and nodded his satisfaction. 'Right,' he ordered the attendant slaves. 'Bandage her and put her to one side. And if I catch any of you messing about with her, I'll geld you with a red hot iron.'

I had started with a score of women, a dozen yet remained to fight. The best—I'd selected them with care. They would fight in two batches of a half-dozen a time, the bouts set between other, more important events. Now as three pairs of *myrmillones* battered at each other with ringing fury, there was time to teach them another lesson.

'Verdalia. Pholis. Claudia. All of you, come with me.'

The area beyond the Gate of Death was a shambles. Dead bodies lay stacked to the sides waiting for later removal; the animals to the butcher's shops, the human to burial pits or pyres.

Blood-smeared slaves, their skins slimed with sweat, watched as I found Helena and showed her to the others.

'Remember her? A nice girl. Who was her lover? You?' I stared at a woman who had tears running down her cheeks. 'Would you like to caress her now?'

'No!'

'Do you want to kill the one who did this? Well, she'll be waiting for you on the sand. Think of Helena when you meet her. All of you think of Helena. Fight and win, or you'll end up like she did—food for the dogs!'

And I would end up a contracted slave, a year of my life forfeited to Fiona for the money I had borrowed, most of which Agonestes had used to back my victory.

He was waiting for us when we returned and he gestured me to one side.

'Something's odd, Atilus,' he said quietly. 'I've been hanging around the place where Helvidius keeps his women. I'll swear that a couple of them, at least, are men.'

'Are you certain?'

'No,' he admitted. 'But I've that feeling. Watch the next time we're out.'

Advice I followed as, to the summons of the trumpets, again I ran with my women into the arena.

Lashing them into battle, snapping advice, running from one to the other of the three under my charge, I watched their opponents. One, a *retiarius*, was suspiciously deft despite the swell of barely formed breasts. A woman has hips broader than those of a man. Her legs are more widely spaced. It affects the way they run, the way they move.

'The net,' I snapped at Pholis. 'Dodge! Now in with the sword! In! Aim for the guts!'

Instructions she obeyed, moving in with quick, jabbing thrusts as I had taught her. Without needing my advice, she moved her head so as to avoid the thrust of the trident, not relying on the lattice protecting her face to save her eyes from the tines. Metal rasped as the points hit her armour, slipping from the overlapping plates covering her right arm and ripping through the skin of her torso just below her breasts.

'In!' My whip stung her rear. 'Move and get him! Fast!'

I moved on as the *retiarius* fell, shouting at another of my women, seeing a third fall. Blood rained from a torn jugular, splashing my face and hair with blood, the warm, sickly stench of it hanging thickly in the air.

Marius, yelling his fury, struck with his lead-weighted thong, Helvidius adding his own blows to a cringing figure facing one of my Nubians.

'Kill!' I yelled. 'Kill!'

Smash down the defence, slam home the trident, pierce the eyeballs, send the points into the brain. Kill and live. Live!

I lost half my women, Helvidius the same, and the score rested to his advantage. As we passed through the Gate of Life Agonestes said, 'Atilus, did you notice?'

'Yes, you could be right.'

'What are we going to do about it?'

'For now, nothing.' A check of the bodies might reveal the truth if any of the disguised men had died, but bribed slaves could make that impossible. 'Let's get a drink.'

We were both worn with our exertions and I was glad of the respite arranged by Julius Asprenas. Now paired Thracians were fighting to please the crowd with an exhibition of trained skill. Then would come some *essedarii*, men fighting from chariots, and after them would come our third bout.

'Eight to six,' mused Agonestes. 'We have to kill five of his to one of ours in order to win. Long odds—I should have waited before placing the bets.'

'We'll win.'

"Not if he sneaks in some more men, we won't.' Agonestes sipped at his wine. 'He must have found some hermaphrodites, and my guess is they came from the east. I've seen men looking just like girls who could fight like demons. They had breasts too. Out there you find some peculiar things.'

Creatures trained and distorted for the degenerate pleasure

of wealthy patrons. Men looking like women which Cossos Bassius could have found and had delivered to Helvidius. Had he learned of my affair with his wife and attempted a subtle revenge?

Again, Gallus Caecina earned the money I had given to him. A word and it was arranged, officials coming to check each of my women. One winked as he explained why he had come.

'Just routine, Atilus. A hint was given that some of the girls aren't what they seem. No reflection on you, of course.'

'And Helvidius?'

'He didn't like it.' Again the wink. 'He had to make a few substitutions. Before we checked, of course, but those passed are under guard. As yours will be.' He looked admiringly at Verdalia. 'Now there's a woman I'd like to guard all my life.'

A sentiment echoed by the crowd as we ran into the sunlight.

The cloud had gone now, and the heat was becoming intense, Verdalia's skin gleaming beneath a thin coating of oil.

I saw Nero lean forward, his eyes searching her nudity, one hand lifted as if to halt the event. Then Poppaea pulled at his arm and, reluctantly he gave the signal to commence.

Twelve women moved forward each intent on the kill.

As *retiarii* I had Verdalia, Claudia, and one of the Nubians. As *secutares* three of the best other than Pholis, who had fought and won, and now watched from the Gate of Life. Three women whom I urged as Agonestes urged the others.

'In!' Antonia was reluctant to face the glittering points of the trident held by her opponent. The sting of my whip encouraged her. 'In!'

Normally each gladiator had his own trainer; the fact that Agonestes and I were forced to handle all of our women added an extra spice. Helvidius and Marius, like ourselves, raced from one to the other, whips busy, voices rising above the scuff of sandals and the ring of steel.

I heard the roar of the crowd, a signal that someone had fallen. Verdalia? There was no time to look. The woman before me was in trouble, her helmet caught in the net, her sword waving as she desperately tried to save her body from the thrust of the trident.

'Take it in the thigh!' I ordered. 'Take it, damn you! Take it and move in!'

Her only chance, hampered as she was by the net. A wound which would freeze the movement of the tines and give her a chance to get in with her sword. A chance she hesitated to take.

'Habet!' The roar was a thunder as she stumbled and fell, blood bright on her side. 'Habet, hoc habet!'

Wounded, down, counted out. As she lifted her arm in surrender I ran to one of the others. The fallen woman was beyond help. Blood gushed from her mouth as the barbs of the trident buried themselves in her lungs.

One down. Another and I couldn't win but only tie. A third and I would have lost.

'Fight!' Fury sent my whip singing through the air. 'Get in and fight, damn you! Fight!'

Fight and win. Defeat and kill. Save your life and gain your freedom. Fight, you bitches! Fight!

Fight and win and save me from a year of slavery!

Responding, she lunged forward. Luck was with us both. The *retiarius* facing her stepping backwards, slipped on a patch of buried blood, and fell to sprawl helpless on the sand.

Death came in seconds.

'Atilus!' The crowd was on its feet, screaming. 'Atilus!'

Dashing sweat from my eyes I looked around. My third *secutor* was holding her own, but the Nubian was down, her eyes open, glazed as they looked at the sun. Between her breasts blood bubbled in a dying fountain.

Beside her lay the woman who had killed her, a Thracian, oozing pits where her eyes had been, blood and slime staining her cheeks. Verdalia had killed her.

And Verdalia had gone insane.

Her screams rose above the roar of the crowd and her face was that of an animal, hatred and blood-lust making her ugly. Her hair, loose, streamed out behind her as, net forgotten, she gripped her trident in both hands as if it had been a spear.

Running to where the *retiarius* who had killed my *secutor* stood, she plunged the weapon into the woman's back before she could turn, ripped free the barbs and, without pause hurled herself at Marius.

'Atilus!' Agonestes came running towards me. 'She's gone berserk!'

It was the madness of her people, the overpowering rage which gripped them, to send them running wild, heedless of wounds and consumed with the desire to kill and kill and keep on killing until they were cut down or until nothing was left to destroy.

Her original opponent, dead, lay with legs straddled her chest an ooze of blood. Claudia's, taken from the side, coughed out her life in a ruby stream. As I watched Marius, trying to dodge, took the trident in his mouth, the barbs smashing teeth, ripping his tongue, driving through to the spine.

Still screaming, Verdalia jerked free the weapon and ran to where Helvidius was standing.

He was ready for her.

From the sand he had snatched a *gladius* and stood poised and waiting. Experienced in the ways of the arena, he knew exactly what to do. As the barbs neared his face he swayed to the right, his left arm rising to hit the shaft and push aside the points. As they flashed over his shoulder he drove the sword in the woman's stomach.

'Verdalia!'

'Atilus!' Agonestes grabbed at my arm as I shouted. 'No! You can't!'

His hand fell away as I raced over the sand, stooping to snatch up a fallen sword. Helvidius raised his own as I came within reach, and metal grated as the blades clashed. He was strong, but I was stronger, driven by a rage which made the weapon a wand in my hand. It smashed down his defence, knocked aside his thrust, and then I was chopping, hacking, blood raining from gaping wounds, a crimson fountain which bathed me with carmine wetness as, before me, a shapeless mass of slashed flesh fell to lie in a puddle of its own blood.

'Verdalia!'

Throwing aside the sword, I knelt beside her. The blade had cut deeply into her stomach releasing blood which stained her crotch, her thighs, the sand on which she lay.

At the touch of my hand she opened her eyes.

'Atilus!' The madness had left her and she smiled as she reached up to touch my cheek. 'I had a dream,' she whispered. 'You and I together with our son.'

'Verdalia! I love you!'

'And I you, my darling. But it's so cold. Hold me close to you. Hold—'

Her hand fell from my cheek as my arms closed round her and her head rolled to one side, the eyes glazed, unseeing.

I had won, the roar of the crowd left that in no doubt. Nero was pleased, laughing as he lolled on his ornate chair, and his favour was assured. I would have money and fame and the adulation of Rome. But all I could see was Verdalia and the blood between her thighs.

AUTHOR'S NOTE

While the actual date when female gladiators first appeared in the amphitheatres is unknown, there is no doubt they did exist, and it is possible that Nero initiated them. Certainly, according to Tacitus, the practice was rife in AD 63, the ninth year of Nero's rule. Juvenal, who died in AD 140, was scathing in his ridicule of women who adopted the profession, especially noblewomen, who apparently liked, as did men of a similar calibre, to participate in various gladiatorial displays. The Emperor Septimius Severus, after a particularly noticeable outbreak of gladiatorial contests between women, forbade female combatants altogether in AD 200.

GLOSSARY

Amatores—Fans of gladiators
Andabatae—Men who were forced to fight blindfolded
Bestiarii—Those who fought wild beasts
Caladarium—Hot room of the baths
Cruppellarii—Gladiators who wore heavy cuirasses
Dimachaeri—Gladiators who fought with two daggers
Domus—A large house or mansion
Duumvir—A provincial official
Essedarii—Gladiators who fought from chariots
Familia—A troupe of gladiators owned by a lanista
Fascina—The trident used by a retiarius
Frigidarium—The cold room at the baths—the plunge
Gladius—Sword—hence gladiator or swordsman
Insulae—Tenement buildings
Lanista—The owner of a group of gladiators
Ludi—Games—a word applied to the entire spectacles in the amphitheatres
Lusiones—Fight conducted with wooden weapons
Maeniana—Stands at the amphitheatres
Missus—Lost
Munera—A gladiatorial display
Myrmillones—Gladiators derived from the original Samnites
Primus palus—A first-class fighter
Prolusiones—Mock fights, usually with whips and shields
Retiarii—Gladiators who fought with a net and trident
Rudis—The symbolic wooden sword presented as an award and

honour to successful and popular gladiators

Secutor—The usual opponent of a *retiarius*

Sica—The curved, scimitar-like sword used by a Thracian

Spectati—A gladiator with one or more successful fights to his credit

Stans missus—A draw

Thracian—A gladiator fighting with a small shield and sica

Tiro—A beginner

Trinqui—Unfortunates condemned to be used as ficial victims and thrown to the wild beasts

Unctores—Masseurs

Veterani—Old hands

ABOUT THE AUTHOR

English writer **E. C. Tubb** is internationally known, having been translated into more than a dozen languages. In a sixty-year writing career he published over 120 novels, and more than 200 science fiction short stories in such magazines as *Astounding/Analog, Authentic, Fantasy Adventures, Galaxy, Nebula, New Worlds, Science Fantasy*, and *Vision of Tomorrow*.

Tubb's early science fiction novels were exciting adventure stories, written in the prevailing fashion of the early 1950s. Yet, from his very first novel, his work was characterized at all times by a sense of plausibility, logic, and human insight. These qualities were even more evident in his short stories, which were frequently anthologized.

By 1956 his output included adventure, detective stories, and westerns, but he remained best known for his numerous science fiction novels, of which *Alien Dust* (1955) and *The Space Born* (1956) were acknowledged classics. Tubb became famous for his long-running "Dumarest of Terra" series of novels, the galaxy-spanning saga of Earl Dumarest and his search to find his way back across the stars to the legendary lost planet where he was born—Earth. They eventually spanned thirty-three titles, the final one, *Child of Earth*, appearing in November 2008. Equally well known were his *Space 1999* TV novelizations, and his "Cap Kennedy" novels. Some of his finest SF short stories were collected in *The Best Science Fiction of E. C. Tubb* (Wildside, 2003). Tubb continued to write dynamic science fiction novels right up to his death in October, 2010.

www.ingramcontent.com/pod-product-compliance
Lightning Source LLC
Chambersburg PA
CBHW022152260626
47155CB00017B/1848